IF YOU DARED TO LOVE A LAIRD

LAUREN ROYAL

February 2022 Edition
FORMERLY TITLED "FOREVERMORE"

IF YOU DARED TO LOVE A LAIRD by Lauren Royal

Published by Novelty Books, a division of Novelty Publishers, LLC, 205 Avenida Del Mar #275, San Clemente, CA 92674

Formerly titled "Forevermore"
Originally published in paperback by Penguin Putnam Inc.

Learn more about the author and her books at www.LaurenRoyal.com.

ISBN: 978-1-63469-152-9

MORE CHASE FAMILY BOOKS

CHASE FAMILY SERIES

When an Earl Meets a Girl

How to Undress a Marquess

If You Dared to Love a Laird

A Duke's Guide to Seducing His Bride

Never Doubt a Viscount

The Scandal of Lord Randal

A Gentleman's Plot to Tie the Knot

A Secret Christmas

A Chase Family Christmas

Alice Betrothed

CHASE FAMILY SERIES: THE REGENCY

Tempt Me at Midnight

Tempting Juliana

The Art of Temptation

For Terri Castoro,
critique partner and friend forevermore.

I couldn't do it without you!

ONE

Village of Cainewood, England
September 1667

*T*HEY'D SENT A carriage to take her to the castle.

In all her thirty-one years, Clarice Bradford had never ridden in a carriage. Gingerly she climbed inside and perched on the leather seat, settling the pink skirts of her Sunday gown.

Dressed in blue to match her eyes, Clarice's five-year-old daughter bounced up and down on the seat opposite. "I've been in this carriage, Mama. When Lord Cainewood brought me to live with you."

In her short life, Mary had been orphaned by the plague and then abandoned during the Great Fire of London. But in the year since Lord Cainewood brought

Mary to her doorstep, Clarice had come to love the girl like her own.

"I remember you climbing out of this carriage. That's one day I'm unlikely to ever forget." Clarice reached across and tweaked her daughter on the chin. "It's a fine carriage, isn't it?"

Mary shrugged, her blond ringlets bouncing on her shoulders in the same rhythm as the vehicle. "I would rather ride a horse."

"That wouldn't be a very elegant way to arrive at a nobleman's wedding."

A sigh wafted from Mary's rosy lips. "I s'pose not." She nibbled on a fingernail until Clarice pulled her hand from her mouth. "Who is Lord Cainewood marrying?"

"I haven't met her, poppet, but if she's marrying Lord Cainewood, she must be a grand lady. I've heard she's from Scotland."

"Scotland. Is that very far away?"

"Far enough." Clarice leaned across the cabin and took Mary's hands in hers. "Can you believe we're going to a wedding at the castle?"

Though Mary smiled, it was clear she wasn't overly impressed. "I lived at the castle before." Last year, after Lord Cainewood's brother had swept her from the fire and brought her to Cainewood. "For a whole month."

"Well, I've only been in the great hall for Christmas dinner once a year," Clarice said. "I've never seen any of the other rooms."

"I'll show you around," her daughter proclaimed, displaying nary a hint of the awe that made Clarice's heart beat a rapid tattoo.

The castle was grandly ancient; the very thought of entering the family's private living space was both daunting and exciting. And the carriage was clattering over the drawbridge already.

Shadows sheathed the carriage's windows as they passed beneath the barbican. Then it was bright again, and Clarice Bradford found herself inside the crenelated walls of Cainewood Castle.

The carriage door was flung open, and Mary ran down the steps into the enormous grassy quadrangle. "Who are you?" Clarice heard her ask. "And who is this?"

"You must be Miss Mary," came a masculine voice. Clarice alighted from the carriage to see a man crouched by her daughter, an infant in his arms. "And this is baby Jewel. Lord Cainewood is an uncle now, aye?"

"Lord Cainewood plays games with me sometimes. The babe is lucky to have him for an uncle." Four stories of stately living quarters looming behind her, Mary ran a small finger down the child's tiny nose. "But Jewel is an odd name. 'Specially for a boy."

"Ah, but Jewel is a lass." A grin appeared on the stranger's face, lopsided and indulgent. "Though she has little hair on her head yet, she's a girl."

"Oh. Will she have hair soon?"

"Aye. A bonnie lass she'll be. Just like you."

Mary's giggle tinkled into the summer air as the man rose to his full height and caught Clarice's gaze with his.

Something stirred inside her when she met his warm hazel eyes. Since he hadn't answered Mary, Clarice had no idea who he was. He looked to be a wedding guest, though, dressed in a fancy blue suit trimmed with bright gold braid. She'd been told this would be a small family wedding. Judging from his accent, he must belong to the bride's side.

The stranger was tall. Clarice was not a short woman, but he topped her by nearly a head. Straight wheaten hair skimmed his shoulders and fluttered in the light breeze, shimmering in the sunshine. And those eyes...she felt she could get lost in them.

She gave herself a mental shake. This magical fairy-tale day was sparking her imagination—that was all. She'd never thought to be inside the castle walls as an invited guest to the lord's wedding—she and Mary the only commoners invited—the only non-family invited, come to that. Lord Cainewood had said that since their misfortune had inadvertently led to his marriage, he wanted them with him to celebrate. The sheer wonder of it was going to her sensible head. Making her giddy.

"You talk funny," Mary said to the stranger.

"Mary!" Clarice exclaimed, but she couldn't seem to look at her daughter. Her gaze was still riveted to the man's. He didn't talk funny, either. To the contrary, the

Scottish cadence of his words seemed to flow right into her and melt her very bones.

Lud, she was afraid her knees might give out.

"Do you think so?" He tore his gaze from Clarice's and looked down at Mary. "Ye should gae a' folk the hearin', ye ken?" he said in an accent so broad it was obviously exaggerated.

At the look on her daughter's face, Clarice laughed, then clapped a hand over her mouth. Surely laughter wasn't appropriate at a lord's wedding. She schooled her expression to be properly sober. "He means you should listen to people without passing judgment," she told Mary.

The man grinned, showing even white teeth. "I'm Cameron Leslie," he said. "Cousin of the bride." Shifting the baby to one arm, he reached for Clarice's hand. When he pressed his warm lips to the back, her breath caught and she thought she might swoon.

Clarice Bradford had never swooned.

"And you two must be the mother and daughter I've heard so much about, whose trials set Cainewood on the road to meet and woo my cousin Cait." She released her breath when he dropped her hand. "Though to hear Lord Cainewood's side of it," Mr. Leslie added with a jaunty wink, "it was Caithren who did the wooing."

Clarice couldn't help but smile. His cousin Caithren sounded like just what serious Lord Cainewood needed. "I'm Clarice Bradford," she said.

"It's pleased I am to meet you." He looked down when Mary tugged on one leg of his velvet breeches. "What is it, sweet?"

"Will you pick me up?"

"Mary!" Clarice frowned and set a hand on the girl's shoulder.

But the man handed the baby to Clarice, then reached down and swung her daughter into his arms. "Of course I'll hold you, princess." His eyes danced with pleasure. "She's charming," he told Clarice.

"I…" She cradled the sweet-smelling babe, at a loss for words. Mary was acting inappropriately forward, to the point of burrowing into the man's neck. And Clarice…

Clarice was *jealous*.

It was absurd. The planes of his face were clean-shaven, his skin flawless and…young. The man was incredibly young. Early twenties, she'd guess. She could see it in his complexion, the straightness of his lanky form, the angle of his head. This was not a man who had yet suffered the slings and arrows of life.

And Clarice was nearly thirty-two years old. Old enough to know she had no business lusting over a young man of any sort, let alone one dressed in the trappings of aristocracy.

She'd never lusted before, ever. It was quite a heady emotion.

Her daughter was clearly just as smitten.

Clarice startled out of her trance when the whine of bagpipes filled the quadrangle.

"That's our signal," Mr. Leslie said. "I expect I should fetch the bride."

When he set Mary on her feet, the girl reached up and firmly took his hand. "May I come with you?"

"Of course you may, princess."

"Princess," Mary breathed as they walked away. Bemused, Clarice smiled down at the cooing infant in her arms, vaguely wondering how she'd ended up holding a marquess's niece. And what she was supposed to do with her.

She glanced up to ask Mr. Leslie, but he was already too distant and Mary was happily chatting away. She wondered if perhaps she'd lost her daughter to this man.

Mary had always dreamed of being a princess.

TWO

 AMERON LESLIE was known to be a wee bit quiet. A man of simple needs, he didn't want for much. But when he did find something he wanted, he generally got it.

At the moment he was wanting Clarice Bradford. Or his body was, at least. His head told him he couldn't come to that conclusion following a five-minute conversation.

Good Lord, he mused as he climbed the steps to his cousin's chamber, in all his twenty-four years he'd never found himself attracted to a woman as he was to Clarice. Her quiet dignity, her wholesome beauty, something in her large gray eyes. The way she so clearly adored her delightful daughter.

A pity his time here in England was so short. He'd

like to get to know the lass, but he had less than a week before he needed to head home to Scotland.

Wondering how much persuading Clarice would take to spend some time with him, he knocked on his cousin's door and called through the sturdy oak to ask if she was ready.

When the door opened, his jaw dropped. "Cait?" Dressed for her wedding, she looked different from the girl he'd known since her birth. Unbound from its customary plaits, her dark blond hair, so much like his, hung straight and loose to her waist. She wore cosmetics and a sky-blue gown trimmed in silver lace. An English gown.

"Good Lord," he said. "Cait, you look lovely."

"Thank you." She smiled, her hazel eyes sparkling as she surveyed his own attire, a deep blue velvet suit that he'd borrowed from one of the groom's brothers. He suspected Caithren thought he looked as English as she. She aimed a curious glance at the wee lassie who still held his fingers gripped tight. "And who is this?"

"Her name is Mary, and she and her mother are special guests. She, uh, attached herself to me." Cam lifted his hand, and Mary's little hand came up with it. Though he gave a sheepish shrug, his heart swelled, warm and pleased. "She may be walking down the aisle with us."

Caithren knelt, her silk skirts pooling around her. "Good day," she said.

"Good day," Mary returned in a small, polite voice. "I am pleased to meet you, my lady."

"I'm not—" Cait started.

"You'll be a lady within the hour," Cam interrupted with a teasing smile. "You may as well get used to it." He knew firsthand how difficult it was to adjust to a new station in life, having unexpectedly found himself to be a baronet after Caithren's brother died last month. He blew out a breath. "I, on the other hand, will never get used to being a sir."

"Aye, you will." Cait stood and linked her arm though his. "Shall we go?"

Bagpipe music swelled when they reached the double front doors and stepped out into the sunshine. It was a glorious day to be wed, the quadrangle redolent with the scent of newly-cut grass, the sky blue as Cait's gown and dotted with wee, puffy white clouds. Cameron's gaze swept the enormous castle's crenelated walls and the ancient keep while he mentally compared it to the tiny castle he'd recently inherited in Scotland. Beyond the timeworn tower, the grass grew high and untamed.

"Gudeman's croft," Caithren murmured.

"What is that?" Mary asked.

Cameron knelt down to her. "A place allowed to grow free as a shelter for brownies and fairies."

"Oh." Mary's eyes opened wide. "Do you know stories of brownies and fairies?"

"Many. But they'll have to wait for later." With his free hand, Cam ruffled her unruly curls, then he stood and faced Cait. "It's really the old tilting yard. Colin told me they don't groom it since it's long been in disuse."

"I knew that." Her lips curved in a soft smile as she scanned her new home. "Can you believe this place, Cam?"

He met her hazel eyes. "You always were meant to live in a castle, sweet Cait."

"Aye," she said, no doubt thinking of her family's tiny castle at home—Cameron's castle now. "But who'd have ever guessed it would be such an enormous, historic one…and in England?"

"You'll do fine." Though they'd always been insepa-rable and he would miss her terribly, Cam knew in his heart she belonged here at Cainewood with the marquess she'd come to love. He leaned to kiss her fore-head, then looked up. "There's your man now."

When her gaze flew to her intended, her face lit at the sight of him. Suddenly Cameron ached for the secu-rity this tall, dark-haired man so clearly enjoyed—a woman to love and a place that truly felt like his own.

A family.

Now that Cait was staying here in England, Cameron felt very alone. A family would be comforting. With several bairns who would grow up and help him make the Leslie estate into everything he and Cait had always dreamed it could be.

Clarice walked over to take Mary by the hand. "It's time," she said gently, and reluctantly the wee lass released her grip on Cam. The girl looked over her shoulder, her blue eyes lingering on him as the woman led her away.

"Her mother?" Cait guessed.

"Aye. Her name is Clarice Bradford. You'll like her." Cameron's gaze followed the two as they walked toward the gatehouse on their way to Cainewood's private chapel. Clarice's rich brown hair gleamed beneath a pink-ribboned straw hat. Her pink dress was simple compared to those of Caithren and the other women, but it suited her perfectly.

Cameron was simple as well.

He turned to take Cait by both hands. "Are you ready?" he asked.

"More ready than I ever thought possible." Smiling at him, she squeezed his fingers. "You know, Mam always said it's better to marry over the midden than over the muir."

"I've heard that said, that it's wise to stick within your own circle." Unbidden, his gaze flicked over to Clarice. "But I'm not sure I believe it."

"I don't believe it, either." Caithren's own gaze trailed to her groom, waiting for her by the barbican. "I reckon even mothers are wrong sometimes."

THREE

"*A* SCOTS FUNERAL is merrier than an English wedding," the very-Scottish bride declared.

The fairytale wedding was speeding past. Clarice dragged her unfocused gaze from the dining room's diamond paned windows to the long mahogany table, set with fine china and crystal she'd seen before only in stories. The stack of marzipaned wedding cakes that had sat in the middle had been reduced to one—hers.

"Thank you." Dazed, she smiled up at the servant removing her supper plate, which was still piled embarrassingly high with the most delicious food she'd ever tasted. As another servant set the cake before her, she sipped yet again from her seemingly never-empty goblet of spiced wine.

No matter how ridiculous she told herself she was

acting, her attention all evening had remained focused on the man beside her. She'd nodded and grinned and drank to all the loudly proclaimed wedding toasts, and now she was feeling lightheaded. Cameron Leslie—*Sir* Cameron Leslie, as it turned out, for she'd learned that he was not only young and charming and gut-wrenchingly handsome, but also a baronet—had flirted outrageously through it all. When he wasn't slanting her heated glances or touching her surreptitiously, he was being attentive to her daughter—a sure way to any mother's heart.

Now they all turned to the beautiful bride as she rose with a scrape of her lattice-backed chair. "Whatever happened to that bagpiper?"

Lord Cainewood shrugged. "I think he's eating in the kitchen." His face seemed to radiate a happiness Clarice had never seen. She was thrilled that her suffering and Mary's hadn't been for naught—while senseless, at least it had played a small part in bringing these two people together.

"Well, would somebody fetch him already?" The new Lady Cainewood moved from the table and shook out her gleaming silk skirts. "I'll be wanting to dance."

Following the others' lead, Clarice stood and listened to the bride's instructions. "Hold hands in a circle, lads and lassies alternating."

Clarice found herself between Sir Cameron and one

of Lord Cainewood's brothers, holding two strange men's hands. Aristocratic men, no less.

Lud, this must be a dream.

"That's it," the bride said. "Now, who has a handkerchief?" When one of the men produced one, she handed it to Sir Cameron. "You take the middle since you know what to do."

Clarice didn't know whether she was relieved or disappointed when Sir Cameron released her to do his cousin's bidding. The piper arrived, and Clarice's mouth gaped open when the bride kicked off her high-heeled blue satin shoes. Laughing, her two sisters-in-law did the same.

"Mrs. Bradford?" Sir Cameron tapped her on the arm. "Are you not going to take off your shoes?"

She looked at the women's silk-stockinged feet and then down to her own, clad in wool stockings concealed by shoes both flat and sensible. Surely she could dance in them. Lud, she wouldn't take them off, regardless. Not in front of Lord Cainewood and all his family.

She shook her head, glad when Mary provided a distraction by pulling off her own little brown shoes and gleefully tossing them into a corner. Laughter erupted all around when her stockings followed.

"Very well." The new Lady Cainewood turned to the piper. "We'll have a reel, if you please."

Around and around they went in time to the rousing

tune, until Sir Cameron came from the center to his cousin. The circling stopped, and he laid the lace-edged hankie in a neat square at her feet. They knelt on either side, and she bestowed him with a kiss on the lips. This met with laughter and Clarice's startled gasp. But she could sense an affection between the cousins that made her heart warm; she wondered how much they would miss each other.

Lady Cainewood snatched up the handkerchief and took her place in the middle. Around they went again, dancing until she chose her new husband. Their kiss was long and deep. Clarice's cheeks went hot, and she averted her eyes, only to find Sir Cameron watching her in a way that made her cheeks burn hotter. Casually his hand slipped around her waist, making her more uncomfortable, and somehow she thought he was enjoying her discomfort. Or rather, his own power in making her so. When his arm dropped and he reclaimed her hand, she wondered if she had imagined it all.

The spiced wine had surely gone to her head.

After much throat-clearing and finally applause, Lord Cainewood finally went into the center, and the circling resumed.

The dancers spun by in a blaze of color. The men wore deep jewel tones, the women mint and plum, and the bride sky-blue. The fabrics were rich and sumptuous, shot through with silver and gold, adorned with ribbons and lace. The ladies' stomachers were enriched with intricate embroidery, their skirts split in front and tucked up to reveal glorious matching underskirts. Clarice's Sunday gown seemed so ordinary in comparison; when the dance paused for another kiss, she had to stop herself from fidgeting with the plain pink linen.

"You look beautiful," Sir Cameron whispered in her ear. She was saved from putting her hand to her cheek when he grabbed it to begin the dance again.

After several more rounds, Mary was picked, and no one was surprised when she selected Sir Cameron. She bestowed her new love with a wet, smacking kiss.

Clarice was the only one who'd yet to be chosen. And it was Sir Cameron's turn again…

But he'd no sooner tapped her on the shoulder when the piper quit the tune. Perhaps it was just as well—her face was likely as pink as her dress. But she heard Sir Cameron's groan of disappointment, and it gave her an odd little thrill.

If she didn't know better…but no, she didn't believe in love at first sight. Long experience—as a young wife in an arranged marriage, and then a widow alone in the world—had taught her not to trust love at all.

And she and Mary were happy together. *Alone* together.

But she was at the castle for this one night… Just this one night, could she not live a fairytale fantasy? Even ever-so-practical Clarice Bradford was entitled to a harmless fantasy now and again, wasn't she?

"A kissing dance!" Her red curls glimmering in the

light of the dining room's fire, Lady Kendra, the groom's sister, breathlessly made her way to a chair. "I've never heard of such a thing!"

"There's much kissing at Scottish weddings." The bride winked at Sir Cameron, who was still hovering close by Clarice. "A kiss can be claimed at the beginning and end of each and every dance." That news made Clarice all tingly inside. "Now, get up, all you lazy-bones. We'll have a strathspey next, and a hornpipe after that."

The strathspey was energetic, a sort of line dance with much weaving in and out—no easy opportunity for kisses there. And the hornpipe was wild. After those, the piper played some lively English tunes, country round dances, until they were all worn out.

Mary curled up on a chair and promptly fell asleep. Finally, when Clarice was certain she'd collapse, the piper launched into a slow, unfamiliar tune.

Sir Cameron took her by both hands and swept her into the dance. But not before claiming one of those before-dance kisses his cousin had mentioned. He leaned close, and his lips brushed hers, light and fleeting, naught more than a whisper.

Her own lips tingled in response, and the kiss left her wanting more. Clarice Bradford, who had never really wanted a kiss from anyone. Her heart pounded with new and not quite welcome feelings. "Wh-what is this dance?" she managed to stammer out.

"A galliard. All the rage at King Charles's court. Or so I've been told. Kendra taught it to me yesterday."

He danced courtly dances, and with the likes of Lady Kendra. Clarice rarely found herself tongue-tied, but she couldn't think of anything proper or significant to say. Not a word. Besides, she was busy watching everyone's stockinged feet as she mimicked their steps.

Sir Cameron's hands felt very warm in hers. She'd never danced a dance designed for a couple—all the country dances she knew were done in lines or a circle. She had to concentrate very hard, and she always felt a beat behind. Step forward on the toes with the left foot. Move the right to meet it and lower the heels.

"Just repeat on the other foot," Sir Cameron whispered.

So far, so good. She was almost enjoying herself.

He squeezed her hands. "Now the same, but twice forward. That's correct."

They came close and then pulled back again. It struck her that the dance was rather provocative, its movements mimicking courtship. Once more her cheeks betrayed her thoughts.

She hated that.

"Do you like it, Mrs. Bradford?"

"It's...difficult."

"You're doing beautifully." He gave her a broad smile that made her heart flip-flop, creasing his faintly-stubbled cheeks.

Dimples. The man had dimples. Her lips curved at the sight.

"Is something funny?" he asked.

"Ah, no. It's just…" The dimples made him look even younger. But she couldn't tell him that. "You're doing beautifully yourself, having learned the dance just yesterday."

"I've many to learn before Friday."

"Friday?"

"Jason—Lord Cainewood—will be hosting a ball to celebrate his marriage. All the local gentry are expected, and some from London as well, I'm told." He sighed theatrically. "Three days to learn a host of dances."

She wished she could see the ball. Not attend it, of course, but just see it, perhaps hiding in the minstrel's gallery. She remembered noticing a minstrel's gallery in the great hall last Christmas Day.

The castle was centuries old and terribly romantic. But other than the great hall, she'd never been inside it before, and odds were she'd never be inside it again. Clarice Bradford did not belong in castles. Which was perfectly all right with her. Tonight was a dream, though, a lovely dream…

"And a week from today I'll be gone."

"Gone?"

The music ended, and the single word seemed to vibrate in the beautiful chamber.

Gone…

Why did the thought make her suddenly sad? She'd only met this man tonight, so surely she wouldn't be missing him.

"Aye, I must get back to Leslie. The harvest approaches." He held on to her hands for a few extra moments before dropping them. "I shouldn't have been away this long, but I couldn't think of missing Caithren's wedding. And then the ball, just a few days more…but after that I must leave."

"Oh." Surely it wasn't proper for her to care about him leaving. She certainly wouldn't admit it.

But he looked like he wanted her to.

Impossible. Wishful thinking was leading her to see something that wasn't there. And regardless, he was too young.

When the music didn't resume, Clarice wasn't sure if she was relieved or disappointed. It was past midnight, and the wedding party began stumbling off to bed with a lot of final kisses and good nights. The women even gave Clarice hugs, which rendered her speechless. Titled ladies hugging her.

One of Lord Cainewood's brothers went off to fetch a footman to see her home. Mary didn't wake when Sir Cameron lifted her and beckoned Clarice to follow him through the castle to the double front doors.

Reluctantly, it seemed, he handed over her daughter and leaned against the doorpost with a faint smile. "It was a lovely evening."

"Yes, it was. Like a dream, almost." In her arms her slight daughter felt limp, warm, and overly heavy. "A beautiful dream of castles and lords and ladies. A fairy-tale come true. And now I must return to the real world, but I'll carry this memory with me."

"I'll remember our dance."

Low and meaningful, his words were like warmed, sweet honey flowing over her. Her own words failed her once again.

He touched her on the arm. "May I see you tomorrow?"

"P-pardon?" She looked down to where his fingers still rested on her pink linen sleeve. Long, strong fingers, so unlike her late husband's older, coarse ones. Beneath the fabric, her skin prickled and the little hairs stood on end.

"May I see you tomorrow?" When he removed his hand, she felt a distinct sense of loss. "I thought perhaps you'd like to come out walking."

It was impossible! The dream was over. No matter that her heart melted when she looked into his eyes—there could be no point in seeing him again. "I have work to do tomorrow."

Mary slumped in her arms, and Sir Cameron leapt to right her, his hands gentle, lingering on her daughter as he smiled and glanced back up at Clarice. "The next day, then?"

"No, I—" She broke off, not knowing what to say.

He pulled away, but not before he brushed the hair from her daughter's face. "You don't want to see me," he said flatly.

She winced as his eyes faded and his mouth settled into a grim, straight line. "No, it's not that, my lord—"

"I'm not a lord, Mrs. Bradford. Only a mere sir."

"Oh. Sir. Well. It's just—" She drew a deep breath and tried again. "I wouldn't be…seemly…for me to be seen about the village with one so…" She looked down at Mary's tumbled curls. "Young."

There, she'd said it. She looked up.

"Do you really think I'm too young?"

Part of her was mortified that she'd said it—in doing so, she'd as much as admitted she thought he was interested in her. Yet the light was back in his eyes. Clearly he didn't consider this objection insurmountable.

But he didn't know about her other objections—ones more deep-seated and not easily brushed aside.

Just then the door opened and a footman presented her with a brief, snappy bow. "Mrs. Bradford? I've been sent to escort you home."

She knew him. John Foster, Mrs. Foster's oldest son. And John Foster knew her, too. Moved to the castle from the village, he was dressed in Cainewood livery and had acquired the manners to go with it.

She could acquire manners, too, if she wanted to. But John Foster belonged here, and she didn't. Not here or anyplace like it.

"Shall we leave, then?" she asked, following him down the steps.

She didn't dare look back. But she knew Cameron Leslie was watching her. *Sir* Cameron Leslie.

And lud, it felt entirely too good to know that.

FOUR

*L*ATE THE NEXT morning, Cameron paused in front of Clarice's white thatched-roof cottage. A colorful profusion of carefully tended flowers bordered the pristine raked path through her tiny garden to the unassuming front door.

What would she think of the small castle in eastern Scotland he'd recently inherited? It was no palace, to be sure, but her cottage would fit onto half of one of its four floors.

He sneezed as he approached the door, then almost fell in when it jerked open unexpectedly and Mary launched herself into his arms. "Oh, Sir Cameron," she gushed. "I didn't know if I'd ever see you again!"

"Did you think I'd abandon my precious Mary?" Charmed, he held the barefoot, pink-cheeked lassie tight, shifting her to balance on a hip as his gaze swept the cheerful one-room cottage.

Her mother was stirring something in the kettle over the fire, something that smelled fruity and sweet. Not half as sweet as her shy smile when she set down the spoon and turned to look at him, though.

"Ah, there you are," he said.

"Whatever brings you here, my lord?" Clarice blushed prettily and wiped her hands on the apron that protected her simple tan dress, then gestured to the kettle. "I told you I was busy today."

He hadn't forgotten that she'd also told him he wasn't to come at all—her failure to mention that was encouraging. "Now, I'm not a lord, Mrs. Bradford. I told you that yesterday."

"Sir—"

"Please call me Cameron." He set Mary on her feet. "As to what brought me here, I just happened to be walking by—"

"Walking?" Clarice looked a bit flustered. He hoped that would keep her from wondering how he'd located her house. "You walked all the way from the castle?"

Humming a careless tune, Mary ran circles around him. He smiled at her indulgently. "And why not? It's not so very far."

"It's just that…well, they usually ride down in a carriage." Clarice pushed back some hair that had escaped her brown plaited bun. "Or on horseback."

"They?"

"The family, I mean." She reached out to stop her daughter's dance, pulling Mary's small body back against her taller one. Like a shield, Cam thought. "Of course, some of those from the village who work there walk, but the family—"

"I'm not the family," he said with a shrug, wishing he could set her at ease.

"But the new Lady Cainewood is your cousin, isn't she?"

"Aye, Caithren is kin. First cousins, and all. But I'm a simple man, Clarice—" He stepped closer. "May I call you Clarice?"

Color flushed her cheeks. Mary squirmed, but Clarice held her tight and nodded.

"Clarice, then. As I said, I'm a simple man. A baronet is yet a commoner, you know, and before last month I wasn't even that, and never thought to be. Until Caithren's brother died—"

"I'm sorry," she said, looking down to her daughter's curly head.

He waved a hand. Although he would never have wished his cousin harm, he and Adam hadn't been close. "Until he died, I had no property to call my own. No prospect of any, either. So you see, I'm naught but a simple country lad."

At the word *lad*, she glanced up and eyed him sharply. He wished he could bite back the word. "A simple country *man*, I mean."

She nodded slowly, but it was clear she didn't agree. She set Mary free and retrieved her wooden spoon. "Why did you stop here?" she asked again.

"I…"

Mary crossed her wee arms. "He promised to tell me a story."

"Did he?" Toying with the spoon, Clarice looked dubious.

"Oh, yes! He said he knows tales of fairies and brownies." The lassie's eyes danced when she looked to Cameron. "Didn't you, my lord?"

"I'm not a lord, Mary."

"But you did promise me a story, yes?"

"Aye. That I did."

A small trundle bed sat in one corner, and Mary flounced her way over and perched on its edge. She crossed her ankles and folded her hands in her lap. "Well, tell me one, then. A tale of fairies and brownies. Or one about a princess."

Failing to hide a smile, Clarice turned back to stir her pot of preserves. "Mary wishes to grow up and become a princess," she told Cam. "Though I tell her that's never to be."

"Princesses live in castles." Back and forth, Mary swung her feet off the edge of the bed. "Mama says I'll never live in a castle, and I may as well get used to the… what is it you say, Mama?"

"The fact." Still facing away, Clarice set down her wooden spoon.

"The fact, yes. That I'll never live in a castle, and I may as well get used to the fact."

"Hmm...I must say I disagree." As he spoke, Cameron stepped closer behind Clarice, close enough that he could smell her own enticing scent over that of the strawberries. With stunning clarity, a sudden picture invaded his mind: these two, a woman and a child, playing outside his castle.

"You could very well end up living in a castle, Miss Mary. Don't let anyone tell you otherwise. Then have you never heard the story of Nippit Fit and Clippit Fit?"

With a small huff of disapproval, Clarice turned toward him, then jumped back when she saw how near he'd come. He whirled to catch her before she could stumble into the fire, steadying her with his hands on her shoulders.

"Nippit who?" Mary asked, clearly delighted.

Her mother's breath caught, her gray eyes wide with embarrassment. He didn't think it was his imagination when those eyes darkened and she shivered.

"Nippit who?" Mary repeated.

With an inward sigh, he dropped his hands and turned to the lass, then couldn't help but smile at her cocked head and avid expression. "Nippit Fit and Clippit Fit aren't people. It's the story of a commoner who became a princess."

"Oooh. See, Mama?" Mary didn't wait for her mother's answer. "Tell me," she said to Cam.

Looking dazed, Clarice walked slowly to the well-scrubbed table and seated herself before a gigantic bowl of strawberries. Cameron trailed in her wake. "In a country far across the sea lived a prince in a grand castle—"

"Was it pretty?" Mary interrupted.

"Aye, very pretty." Without waiting to be invited, he pulled out another of the four wooden chairs and sat beside Clarice. "It was full of lovely furniture, beautiful artwork, and rare ornaments. One of them was a wee glass shoe which would fit only the most delicate foot in the kingdom."

Mary's feet ceased their swinging motion. "Like mine?" She stared down at her tiny pink toes.

While Clarice pointedly ignored him and worked at hulling her strawberries, he leaned across the table and craned his neck, pretending to peruse the wee lass's foot. "Why, a dainty little foot like yours exactly. And the prince, he loved dainty maidens, he did, and he decided he wouldn't marry until the day he found a maiden who fit the shoe." Under the cover of clearing his throat, he scooted his chair a wee bit closer to Clarice's. "That lucky lady would become his wife."

"And then she'd be a princess," Mary said.

"Aye, that she would. So the prince called one of his knights and gave him the task of riding back and forth across the kingdom until he found a lady the glass shoe would fit."

"And did he find one?"

"Patience, Miss Mary. You must listen to what happened." Wondering if perhaps he should also practice patience, but unable to help himself, he touched her mother on the arm. "Is that not so, Clarice?"

Startled, she looked up and met his eyes. "Patience, yes." Her gaze flicked to where his fingers rested, and when he didn't remove them, she took a strawberry from the bowl and pushed it into his hand.

Clever lass, he thought, pleased and amused.

Mary's feet resumed swinging again. "So what happened?"

"The knight rode back and forth and forth and back, all around the kingdom, summoning all the ladies to come try on the shoe." He popped the small berry into his mouth. "When word got out that whoever could fit it would be the prince's bride, you can wager that every lady in the land begged to try it on." As he swallowed, his own shoe met Clarice's beneath the table.

"And did it fit any ladies?"

"Well, not for the longest time. Try as they might, no ladies could fit their feet into the little glass shoe. Even those who prided themselves on their dainty feet went away in tears."

Clarice moved her foot away…and then, very slowly, she slid it back. Not daring to sneak a glance at her,

Cameron focused on her daughter instead. "Until one day when the knight came upon a house where a laird had once lived—"

"A laird?" Mary's blue eyes looked puzzled. "What's a laird?"

"A Scottish lord, more or less." When she nodded, he went on. "But the laird had died, and his fortune was gone, so his wife and two daughters worked hard to put food on the table and clothing on their backs."

"Were they beautiful, the daughters? And pleasant, as befits a princess?"

"One of them was bitter and cross at the bad luck that had befallen them. But the younger one was always happy and sang as she went about her hard work. A wee lass she was, a bonnie, sweet thing."

"Like me?" Mary asked.

Clarice stifled a laugh.

Cameron's lips twitched as Mary flung herself back onto the bed so that she stared up at the smoke-stained ceiling. "Aye, very much like you."

"So what happened?"

"When the knight rode into their courtyard holding forth the shoe, the older lass ran forward to try it on. But the younger one didn't."

"Why is that?" Mary queried the ceiling. She raised a hand into the air, squinted up, and traced the path of a distant beam with one wee finger. "Did she not want to be a princess?"

"She guessed her feet were small enough to fit the shoe, but she couldn't imagine herself as the wife of a prince. She thought people would make fun of her and say she wasn't fit to be a princess, so she decided it was better to keep back and not even try on the shoe."

"I wouldn't think that," Mary declared.

Clarice looked up from her work. "No, you wouldn't, poppet. But you should. You should learn your place in the world."

"Nay, she shouldn't," Cam disagreed. "Her place is what she makes it, as is yours. We are none of us born to a single destiny—I'm living proof of that."

Clarice's hands worked faster. "Not all of us are so lucky."

"You might find yourself lucky someday." His fingers reached to trail one busy arm.

She stilled at the touch. "I *am* lucky. I have Mary." She smiled at the wee lass. "That is luck enough for me —I have no dreams of living in castles."

"Well, I do." Mary rose from the trundle and dragged another chair out to sit across from Cameron.

Reluctantly he pulled back his hand. It wouldn't do to court the mother in the daughter's clear sight.

Mary knelt on the chair and laced her little fingers together on the tabletop. "What happened to the daughters?"

"The knight gave the glass shoe to the older lass, who carried it up to her bedchamber. Some time passed, until, to the surprise of all, she came back down the stairs with the shoe on her foot."

"Did it truly fit?"

"Well, not exactly. She walked with a wee limp and her face was white as a puffy summer cloud. But only her little sister noticed, and she kept quiet."

Mary shook her head, clearly disapproving of the little sister.

Cameron shared a smile with Clarice. "The knight was so happy to find a lady who fit the shoe, he jumped on his horse and rode to the castle to tell the prince. The next day, the prince gathered his courtiers, and they all rode together to meet and take home his bride."

"Did he fancy her?"

"Well, there was some excitement, I expect you'll imagine, when the prince's party arrived. Though they were poor, the mother gathered all the food she could find for a feast. The selfish sister didn't help at all, but went to her chamber to don whatever fine clothes she could find to impress the prince. When all was ready, the younger sister didn't come to the table, but hid herself instead. She knew that her foot was the smallest in the house—aye, maybe in the kingdom—and she worried that if the prince saw her it could ruin her sister's plans."

"But the prince saw her anyway, didn't he?"

"Nay, for she hid herself well, behind an enormous black cauldron in the courtyard. The prince and his courtiers had a merry evening with many toasts to the couple. And when it was all over, the bride-to-be rode away with him on his horse, so full of pride she didn't bother to say her farewells to her sister and their mother."

Mary climbed from the chair to hug Clarice around the knees. "Not even to her mother?"

When Clarice bent her head to kiss her daughter's curly blond crown, Cameron was sure he'd never seen as touching a picture as the two of them together.

"Not even to her mother." He paused while Clarice drew Mary up to sit on her lap. "But not long after they set upon the road, a wee bird sang from a tree. He trilled, 'Nippit fit and clippit fit, behind the prince rides, But pretty fit and little fit, ahint the cauldron hides.'"

"Oooh…" Mary's blue eyes grew wider. "There is the name of the tale!"

"Aye. And the prince cried, 'What is this that bird doth say?' You can guess he wasn't truly happy with the bride his knight had found for him. He asked, 'Have you a sister, madam?'"

"Did she tell him?"

"To her credit, she didn't lie."

"Mama says I must never lie."

"She is wise, your mama. My aunt used to say, 'Tell the truth an' shame the deil.'"

The lassie cocked her head. "The deil?"

"The devil, aye? It means you should always tell the

truth. The older sister didn't lie, but she told the prince in a whisper, 'My sister is only a very wee one.'"

"Did he hear her?"

"Aye, for he was listening hard for the answer he hoped to hear. 'We will go back and find this wee sister,' he told his courtiers, 'for when I sent forth the shoe, I had no mind that the wearer should nip her foot and clip her foot in order to make it fit.'"

"Ouch!" Mary yanked a stem off a berry, and, making a proper mess of it, stuffed it into her mouth.

"Ouch, indeed." He reached to wipe some berry juice from her chin. "They all turned around and rode back to the house, where the bonnie younger lass was found behind the cauldron. 'Give her the shoe,' the prince told the older sister, and when she took it off, they all gasped to see that she had clipped off part of her toes to get it on."

A grimace on her face, Mary reached beneath the table to grasp her own tiny toes. "Did the shoe fit the little sister?"

"It fit perfectly, and she'd no need to cut her toes, either." He grinned at Mary's giggle. "When the prince saw that it fit, he took the older sister off his horse and put the younger one there instead. And they rode to his castle for the wedding."

"A big castle, and a wedding like yesterday." Mary sighed, her eyes lit with memory. "Was it beautiful?"

"I'm sure it was."

"And did they live happily ever after?"

"Of course they did. For a hundred years and a day."

"A hundred years?" Clarice handed Cameron another strawberry. "You'll put even more dreams in my daughter's head."

The daughter in question hopped down from her mother's lap and made her way around the table to clamber onto Cameron's lap instead. "There's nothing wrong with dreaming," he told Clarice over Mary's curly head.

"I once was a dreamer," Clarice said softly. And her eyes told him that her dreams were long dead.

"You have dreams," Mary disagreed. "In the night, sometimes I hear you dreaming."

"I suspect those are more like nightmares," Cameron said dryly.

A knock came at the door, and Mary jumped from his lap to answer it, squealing with delight when she saw a small, dark-haired girl. "Anne!" She turned to Clarice, her big blue eyes wide with hope. "Mama? Please, can I play? Oh, please?"

"Run along, poppet," Clarice said. "You can finish your chores later."

The door banged shut, and she turned to Cam with a motherly shake of her head. Then she blushed suddenly. "You must leave," she murmured. "It's unseemly for us to be alone."

When he made no move to depart, she bent her head

back to her bowl of strawberries. A spell passed where all he could hear was the liquidy sound of her work, the soft sigh of her breath, and the beat of his own heart in the still room.

"You really must leave," she repeated at last. "As it is, I'll be spending all night convincing my daughter she won't be trying on a shoe and ending up in a castle."

"But, Clarice, I live in a castle. Though it's nothing like Cainewood, more's the pity." He raised her hand and kissed it softly, making her eyes widen. Good Lord, he loved her unique combination of straightforwardness and seeming innocence. "I'm wondering if I could persuade you to accompany me home to see it."

She tried to pull her hand away, but he held tight. Her cheeks flushed pink. "You're jesting."

"Maybe." She looked so pretty when flustered, he couldn't resist teasing her a wee bit more. "But one never knows what the future may bring."

Her mouth dropped open, and she gave a little huff of disbelief. Taking pity on her, he set her hand on the table and patted it comfortingly. "May I see you again tomorrow, Clarice?"

"Tomorrow?" she echoed, looking dazed.

He nodded and stood. "I won't put your reputation at jeopardy by staying here with you alone," he said, making his way toward the door. "But I'll come tomorrow, and together we'll decide if I'm jesting or not."

Without waiting to see her reaction, he slipped

outside, letting loose a resounding sneeze as he made his way through her garden. Whistling tunelessly as he walked back to the castle, he wondered if he'd been jesting at all.

FIVE

*T*HE NEXT DAY, Clarice returned from her morning errands to find Cameron sitting on the low stone wall in front of her cottage, looking altogether too good for her comfort.

Beneath a jaunty brown hat, his hair ruffled in the breeze. Her husband's hair had been a coarse gray, but Cameron's was a silky mixture of blonds and browns. As she imagined running her fingers through it, her hand tightened around Mary's, and she realized she'd thought about him all the night and morning.

Whatever was happening to her? It had to stop.

Her daughter broke from her grasp and went skipping down the lane, straight into Cameron's arms. He stood and swung her in a wide circle, clearly delighting in her high-pitched squeal. Holding a basket heaped with strawberries, Clarice couldn't help smiling as she came near.

It wasn't stopping.

He stilled and held Mary close, his nose in her blond curls, and Clarice guessed he was enjoying her daughter's charming, childish scent. She'd never imagined a man would appreciate a thing like that.

"I've a mind to go rowing on the river," he told Clarice.

"Oh." She looked down at the toes of her neat black shoes. "I hope you'll enjoy yourself."

"I meant with you," he said, making her glance up.

His lopsided grin displayed those dimples that made a giggle want to bubble out of her. But Clarice Bradford didn't giggle.

"And Mary, of course," he added as he set her on her feet.

"I want to play with Anne," Mary said. "I told her we could play with my doll this morning. Mama made me a most lovely doll," she told Cameron.

"Did you truly tell Anne such a thing?" Clarice started toward her door. "You knew that today you're to salt and mold the butter."

Mary's cheeks went pink. "I forgot." Cam sneezed as he followed them through the garden. "Please, Mama?" she asked, shutting the door behind them.

Cameron would never have found it in him to deny the wee lass, but Clarice looked resolute. Mary turned to him, her eyes sparkling with mischief. "Would you mind very much taking Mama rowing without me? Only because I promised Anne."

Was the little minx plotting to get him and Clarice alone together? "I'll miss you," he told Mary with a broad smile, "but nay, I wouldn't mind. It's important to keep your promises."

"The butter—" Clarice started.

"I'll do it later, Mama. I promise, like I promised Anne. She's waiting." The blue eyes begged. "Please?" she repeated.

Cameron saw Clarice's features soften. "Very well. I'll walk you to the cookshop." She put the basket on the table. "But as for going rowing alone with Sir—"

"We'll be out in the open for the world to see," he rushed to reassure her. "There's nothing unseemly about that."

While Mary skipped to her trundle to fetch her doll, Clarice lifted an enormous pile of colorfully decorated throw blankets, holding them before her as though she hoped they were armor Cam couldn't pierce.

"May I see one?" he asked.

"Certainly." She lifted her chin from the top of the stack and he took one and shook it out. "Crewel work," she explained. "They fetch a pretty penny in London."

"You're very talented with a needle." The designs were lovely. "Were you thinking to take them to London now?"

Musical laughter filled the room, lifting his heart. "I've never been to London. Martinson—the village blacksmith—he visits his sister there twice a year and sells them for me." She replaced her chin on the pile. "I heard he's leaving next week, so I thought to deliver them now. The smithy is beside the cookshop."

"Anne's mama owns the cookshop," Mary put in.

"Ah, I see." Cameron followed them to the door. "Do you mind if I walk along with you? I could carry some for you."

"As you wish." Clarice visibly relaxed when he relieved her of more than half the pile. "But I'm not going rowing."

SIX

*H*ALF AN HOUR later, Clarice was stepping into a well-used rental rowboat. Warm sunshine glinted off her plaited brown bun as she seated herself on the wooden bench and settled her pale yellow skirts about her. Cameron took up the oars and paddled them into the center of the River Caine, where the gently flowing water took over the work, drawing them downstream.

"A lovely day, isn't it?" He set down the oars and swept off his hat, tilting his face to the sun with an appreciative sigh. "I'd wager it's raining now in Scotland."

"Do you think so?"

"Aye." He moved to sit beside Clarice, one hand near to hers where it was clenched on the edge of the bench. "A good bet, as it's usually raining. Though it's beautiful for all of that." England was pretty, especially here by the river, but he preferred the more striking, harsh contours of his homeland. Inching his hand closer, he linked his little finger with hers. "Scotland is a bonnie place to live."

Without pulling her hand away, she stared straight ahead, feigning interest in a pair of swans floating on the river. "I'm certain Scotland is lovely. But so very far from here."

"Not so far." He twined another finger with hers. "Caithren has already promised to pay a visit next summer."

"But she's from there, isn't she? She would want to go home."

"Her home is here now, with her husband. As it should be." A quick bit of maneuvering, and three of his fingers were wrapped about a like number of hers. "But aye, she'll want to come see me and keep an eye on what I've wrought with the land of our forebears."

Her hand felt cool, her fingers slightly roughened from her work. More evidence, had he not known it already, that she stood on her own two feet and did what had to be done.

He wanted a woman who would shoulder her fair share of the never-ending tasks around Leslie. His cousin Caithren was like that, and the more time he spent in Clarice's company, the more he found himself thinking she was the same sort of woman. The sort of woman who would be a helpmate and a friend as well as a wife.

He blinked at that thought. "Has the village always been your home?"

"Always. I've never once laid my head anywhere else." She shot a swift glance to their joined hands. "I was born here in Cainewood...more than thirty years ago."

Cameron didn't miss the falter in her voice. "And you're thinking that's a long time, are you?"

She pulled her hand away and folded it with the other one in her lap. "I'm nearly thirty-two. How old are you?"

"Twenty-four," he said, shifting on the bench to face her.

Her eyes grew hazy, contemplative...disappointed? "Just as I thought," she said, drawing a deep breath. "I appreciate your attentions, Sir—"

"Cameron. Just call me Cameron."

Clarice hesitated. While she didn't want to anger him by ignoring the request, she didn't want to encourage him, either. A small part of her had hoped he only *looked* youthful, that he was her age or maybe just a year or two younger.

But twenty-four! Lud, she was eight years his senior!

And a widow with a child.

"I appreciate your attentions," she repeated, omitting the *Sir* this time. "It's quite flattering under the circumstances—"

"And what circumstances might those be?"

She averted her gaze, but the yellow buttercups that dotted the riverbank looked entirely too cheerful. "I'm nearly a decade older than you."

"A slight exaggeration," he said. "And you've lived your entire life here in Cainewood. I reckon I've seen more of the world."

"What does that have to do with—"

"I assure you, Clarice, the difference in our ages doesn't matter."

For the first time, she sensed an impatience in him that should have frightened her, given her background. But for some odd reason, it didn't. Or not much.

She drew herself up. "How about my feelings, sir? Do they matter?"

"Of course your feelings matter." Leaning near, he captured her gaze with his. "But maybe you'll find that I can change them."

He was close, so close. Too close. She couldn't breathe. With a straight face, this man—this baronet— was flirting with her.

It was insane.

And even more insane, part of her wished he was serious.

Her heart fluttered as it hadn't since her all-too-short youth. Evidently the fairytale hadn't ended yet. But it would, and then she would fall back to Earth, hurt again by a man.

Because that was what men did to women.

Somehow, she managed to find air. "You cannot just wish my feelings different—"

He silenced her with a kiss that stole her breath again, along with her words. A sweet brush of his mouth that weakened her knees with its tenderness. When he pulled back, she stared at him, silent.

His eyes darkened with concern. "Is something amiss?"

"Your lips are soft," she murmured. She'd never known a man's lips could be soft. Her husband's sure hadn't been.

Cameron's gentle smile warmed her. "So are yours."

"But—"

"Hush." His mouth touched hers again, more insistent this time. His arms slid around to pull her close, and she scooted along the bench until her body was pressed tightly to his. On their own, it seemed, her hands crept up and stole around his neck, meshing themselves in the silky-softness of his shoulder-length hair.

She was lost in a whirl of sensation. As his lips moved over hers, she abandoned herself to the feeling. So strange, so thrilling, so wondrous…

So improper.

She pulled away, glancing about, relieved to find

they'd drifted far enough downstream that no one else was in sight. "I—"

"Hush," he said again, grabbing her back to him and pressing his forehead against hers.

She stared into his eyes, so very close to hers, sensing in their depths an earnestness and an honesty she'd never before seen in any man. But it was only because he was so young. He hadn't experienced the way life could bruise and batter, not just the body but also the spirit.

"You liked that," he said, his tone leaving no space for her to argue. "So why are you trying to escape?"

"I'm not." She tried to shake her head, but only succeeded in rubbing noses. Lud, even that felt good. "I just...I only...well, you surprised me, is all."

"I want to take you home with me, Clarice Bradford. I told you so yesterday."

"You were jesting," she breathed, trying not to hope he hadn't been.

His lips grazed hers again, and she closed her eyes, then released a little whimper when he deprived her of their warm caress.

A low laugh escaped his throat. "Aye, you like it. And I'm not so sure I was jesting."

Before she could react to that, his mouth met hers once more, with a fiery possession that sent the blood racing through her veins. When his lips coaxed hers apart, she was helpless to resist. His tongue swept inside, hot and emphatic, yet still gentle in his way. She paused in shock and then tentatively reached her own to touch it, reveling in the new sensations.

It seemed a long time before he pulled back. As she fought to catch her breath and regain her senses, he caressed her cheek with the backs of his long fingers. "You're an innocent," he murmured, his hazel eyes growing murky. "But you cannot be. You have a daughter, a lovely bright daughter such as I've never seen."

"I didn't give birth to Mary," she admitted softly. "She was brought to me an orphan, a year ago, by Lord Cainewood. But I'm not innocent. I was married fourteen years. And…" She looked down, her gaze settling on the bottom of the old boat.

He touched her hand. "And you were nearly raped, is that what you wanted to tell me? You needn't say the words. I've learned from Caithren what happened—your sorry tale that brought her new husband out for justice and into her arms. Lord Cainewood blames himself, as I understand it."

"It wasn't his fault, though I reckon he may feel responsible. The man was out to hurt him and mistakenly thought he could do it through me. He thought"—she pushed at one of the oars with the toe of her shoe, then looked up at him—"he thought I was Lord Cainewood's mistress."

He rubbed a thumb under her chin. "You're certainly pretty enough."

She wasn't used to compliments—not from the men in her life. The truth was, she didn't know how to respond to them. So she didn't. "The man would have finished the job he'd started, except for what happened to Mary."

"Which was?"

"She was in his way. So he slammed her against a wall. When she lay there, still as death, he took off, afraid he'd killed her."

"Which he almost did, from what I've been told."

She nodded gravely. "She didn't awaken for weeks. But she's better now."

"Thank God for that."

"I do," she said in a whisper. "Every day." From the look in her eyes, Cameron didn't doubt it. "But the truth is that now I'm healed I don't think of my own ordeal overmuch…it was nothing that hadn't happened to me before."

He'd known it somehow, but he wanted to hear it from her lips. "Before?"

"Within my marriage."

He was silent for a long moment before he reached two fingers to lift her chin. "It's sorry I am for you, Clarice. I'm sorry you were hurt, this last time and the times before. And I'm sorry because…I don't understand. As a man, I don't think I'll ever understand."

"You understand very well," she said, wonder in her voice.

Cameron moved away, giving her the space he sensed she needed. "Tell me about your marriage."

"I was fifteen." She focused down at her hands clasped in her lap. "My folks had other mouths to feed. Will needed a wife, children. He was getting on in years —forty-five, he was—and he wanted to breed a family to support him in his dotage."

"Your parents married you off to a man thrice your age?"

She looked up, her eyes flashing with challenge. "Is that so different from what you're asking?"

He gazed at her unblinkingly. "Aye. It is."

For a moment, that challenge persisted. He admired her for that spirit. He'd never wanted a pliable woman.

At length a long sigh escaped her lips. "It's the done thing. I was a good daughter. I offered no argument." She shrugged. "I spent my childhood working my hands to the bone in their home. I thought marriage would be easier."

"But it wasn't."

"Not with Will. All I wanted was a family of my own, a family I could do better with, children I could cherish. But…"

"What?" He leaned to touch her clasped hands. "Tell me."

"Will couldn't give me that." Her voice broke, and she paused for a breath. "He betrayed our vows with other women, and he never gave them children, either."

A beat of silence stretched between them. And then, "Marriage doesn't have to be like that, Clarice. Painful and empty and childless." Rushing on, he took her hands in his and squeezed. "It wouldn't be like that with me."

"Marriage! You're jesting again." But he looked uncertain, surprised by his own words, and Clarice was afraid he mightn't be jesting, after all. "Even were I to take you seriously, and our age difference aside, sir, the fact remains that Mary and I are better off alone. In all my life, I've never been happier than I am now...and I don't mean to change my circumstances."

Without a word, he trailed one finger alongside her face, and her cheeks heated even as she tightened her jaw.

And her resolve. "No matter what my body tells me, my head knows what's best."

He held her hands between his. "You speak of your body and your head. But what does your heart tell you, Clarice?"

Birds twittered in the background while she searched his face, a face smooth and unlined, unmarred by the countless frowns and endless anger that had so characterized the only man she had lived with as a wife.

He'd asked what her heart told her, but she didn't trust it now. "My heart is not at issue here. I—I cannot marry you, Cameron. You're...you're a baronet, for heaven's sake!" She struggled until he let loose her hands. "I cannot marry a baronet."

A new protest. Cameron wondered if it was progress or a step back. "Whyever not? You sound like the little sister."

"Who?"

"The little sister, from the story of Nippit Fit and Clippit Fit. She knew her feet were small enough they might fit the shoe, but she couldn't imagine herself as the wife of a prince. Do you remember? She thought people would make fun of her and say she wasn't fit to be a princess."

Clarice remained mute.

"Don't sell yourself short, love. You're fit to be a queen. It's sorry I am that I can only make you a mere Lady."

The boat rocked violently when she stood. "This is not a fairytale, and I'm not the little sister. These big feet won't fit into any glass shoes. I'm tall, not dainty. Too tall—"

"You're not too tall for *me*." He stood as well, to demonstrate, and the boat swung even more. She swayed wildly. Alarmed, he grabbed for her, but she leapt away.

And flailed backward, headfirst into the river.

SEVEN

*C*AMERON DOVE in after Clarice, clasping her close when she came up sputtering.

"Lud!" She laughed, a sound of pure delight that shocked him out of his wits. He'd expected her to be furious. "You're turning my life upside down, Cameron Leslie. Literally."

The water was frigid, and her teeth were already chattering, her lips turning a decided shade of blue. There was only one thing to do.

Kiss the warmth back into them.

He dragged her against himself, treading water while he pressed his mouth to hers. He was shocked a second time when she cooperated fully. Her arms wrapped around his shoulders, her legs around his waist. He was certain he'd never felt anything as glorious as this willowy, wet woman fused to him, her every curve melding against his body as though they'd been made for each other.

They kissed long and deep, until he realized they were slowly drifting downstream—and the boat was drifting faster. "Hell."

"Wh-what?" Her voice sounded drugged and dreamy.

With a heartfelt groan, he kissed her again, thrilling when her tongue entered his mouth of her own volition.

He could kiss her forever, except he had a feeling it would swiftly lead to other things. Not to mention they would soon be down the river without a boat. He wouldn't mind walking back, but he *would* mind paying for a rickety boat he wouldn't even hold in his possession. Leslie Castle was bonnie, but the estate itself was cash poor.

"Hell," he repeated, pulling back.

"What is it, Cam?"

Cam. He had to reward her for that with another kiss.

"Hell," he said again a couple of minutes later.

"Do you always curse so much?"

"Only when my boat is floating away."

"Lud!" She looked around wildly. And then, "I cannot swim!"

She hung on to his back as he struck out for the boat. Not too long afterward, he hauled himself aboard and pulled her in after him. She sprawled on the bench, laughing. Until she looked down at her wet gown plastered against her front.

With a gasp, she crossed her arms over full, round breasts with rosy peaks that had shown through the transparent pale yellow fabric. "Tell me you didn't see that."

"I didn't see that." But he had. Her breasts were beautiful. Everything about her was beautiful. Not only the way she looked, but her beautiful soul. And the beautiful way she felt in his arms.

She shivered. "I...I don't know what came over me."

"It was the cold," he said, offering her an out. "And the wet."

But they both knew that something had changed in the water.

"Yes, it must have been," she said. Her hair had come undone and hung in long, wet tendrils down her back. He wanted to wrap his hands in it. Her arms were still crossed over her chest. "I'm sorry," she added.

"For what?"

"For making you get wet. Ruining your clothes and boots. I hope..." She froze, and her face went white—whiter than the cold could possibly warrant. "Please don't be vexed with me."

"Why would I be vexed with you, Clarice?"

She looked like she expected him to be cross, and the truth was, that expectation in itself raised his ire. He wanted to kill the man who had taught her to be so wary.

Lucky for him, the bastard was already dead.

"You didn't do it on purpose," he said. "And truth be told, I would happily ruin my boots to hold you again." He moved closer. "May I kiss you again, Clarice?"

She bit her lip, for all the world looking like she didn't believe him.

He wouldn't push her, not now when she looked so cold and miserable. Moving to the other bench, he sighed and picked up the oars. With strokes made powerful by frustration, the boat was soon slicing through the water toward the docks.

"Tell me, Clarice," he asked presently, "if you cannot swim, why weren't you frightened when you fell?"

Her words were long in coming, and when they finally did, it was with a kind of wonder, as though she surprised herself with her answer. "I knew you would come after me," she said simply.

Progress, he decided. It would have to do for now.

EIGHT

"*I*'M THINKING..." The horse in the stall before him flicked its tail, and Cameron forced his mind back to the discussion. "I'm thinking if I cross our Highland ponies with some of this stock, then—"

"Why're you hanging around here, Cam?" Caithren grinned and took her cousin's hand, pulling him out of Cainewood's stables. "It's obvious your head is somewhere else."

"I wanted to study English breeding methods." He followed her along the path back to the castle. "And the estate manager's theories pertaining to crops—why, there are all sorts of newfangled ideas that bear exploring, as long as I've taken the time to remain here in England until—"

"Cam." Caithren paused on the trodden grass that

led through a meadow sprinkled with yellow butter-cups, her smile all too knowing. "You don't want to talk about crops."

"Nay?" Cameron sneezed, then rubbed a finger under his nose. "Do you know, then, who around here might be considered the expert on sheep—"

"You're not wanting to talk about sheep, either."

He remained mute, cocking one sandy brow.

"You've been distracted all afternoon," she declared. He never had been able to hide much from Cait. "Would you rather be somewhere else?"

"Nay. Nay, of course not." He almost reached to tug one of her plaits—an old gesture of affection between them—before remembering she now wore her hair loose to please her husband. He crossed his arms instead. "How is married life treating you, Cait?"

"So far I like it." She turned and started ambling over the drawbridge, her long, straight hair fluttering in her wake. "Very much," she called back, laughter in her voice.

Behind her, his boots sounded loud on the timeworn wood. "I'm going to miss you." They'd been there for each other, always. "I can hardly imagine returning to Leslie alone."

"You need someone to share it with." Exactly what he'd been thinking, but he could all but hear the wheels turning in her head. And they weren't running the same direction his did. "There is always Lady Nessa."

"She wouldn't have me when I was plain Cameron Leslie—"

"But now you're the laird, Cam." Caithren stopped beneath the barbican and turned to him.

"Exactly." He blinked at her in the shadows. "Whatever feelings I had for Nessa died when she laughed at my proposal. She is sleekit, but cold underneath, aye? I won't be going back to her now."

His gaze drifted up to the massive portcullis overhead. The iron-banded gate would kill him instantly should it fall. Indeed, he would prefer such a fate to life with Lady Nessa.

"And the village lasses?" She grinned and started walking again, backward this time, avidly watching his face. "I can think of more than a couple who are anything but cold. You've shared a tumble or two with some of them, aye?"

He should have seen something like that coming. He reached for her shoulders and spun her to face away. "I won't be saying." There were some things he didn't share, not even with Caithren. "But there's none of them I can picture spending my life with, regardless." He followed her into the quadrangle and up the winding stairs of the old keep, all the while picturing spending his life with a certain woman who waited in a small white cottage. "I want somebody like Clarice—I mean, Mrs. Bradford."

His statement seemed to vibrate through the ancient

stones, and his cousin's feet faltered on the steps. "You mean you want Clarice herself, don't you?" He could hear the smile in her voice as she climbed. "Don't trouble yourself to argue—I saw you two together at my wedding. Does it not bother you that she's been married before?"

"If I were thinking of having her, nay, it wouldn't bother me." They passed beneath an archway and onto a long stretch of wall walk that circumnavigated much of the castle. "She didn't have an easy time of that marriage, Cait. Not that I'm planning to take her home with me, you understand, but it's the truth I've found myself wondering if maybe I could make her happy. And Mary. She's a precious lass, and she's had a hard life."

It was quiet up on the wall, and the view stretched for miles, lush and green. "You shouldn't marry someone to right past wrongs," Cait said softly. "Or even to make her happy. You should marry for your own reasons. If marriage is what you're implying you want, you need selfish reasons, if I may say so."

"I have my own reasons. But they don't matter, since Cl—Mrs. Bradford—won't consider my suit. Not that I've been trying to court her. That would be daft, would it not? I'm leaving in four days." He crossed to the side facing the castle. "She thinks she's too old for me."

Though Caithren remained on the other side, he

could feel her gaze on his back. "What do *you* think, Cam?"

"I think she's lovely and sweet, and a strong woman who isn't afraid of hard work. Life at Leslie isn't easy, as you well know. It's no Cainewood." With the sweep of an arm, he gestured at the immense edifice of the castle and the open quadrangle, continually crisscrossed by servants going about their business. As castles went, Leslie and his lifestyle there couldn't have been more of a contrast. "My wife won't be lying around eating sweetmeats all the day."

When he turned to face her, Caithren's eyes flashed hazel fire. "Is that what you think I'll be doing?"

He raised both hands in mock self-defense. "I know you better than that. But the fact remains you could do nothing more than that if it pleased you. Whereas *my* wife—"

"You *are* thinking of marriage, aren't you?"

"I think I might love her," he said simply, shocked at his own admission but knowing it was true. "That's reason enough to marry her, aye?"

Cait came over and rested a hand on his shoulder. "Are you sure, Cam? You've known her but a few days."

For a spell, he just measured her. "And how long did you know your new husband before you decided you love him?"

She inclined her head in a thoughtful nod. "Point

conceded. Maybe the Leslies just fall fast." She could hardly say otherwise, since her own romance had culminated in a marriage proposal within less than two weeks. "So then I have a question for you, Cameron Leslie." She grinned. "Why have you wasted the afternoon hanging around here when you could be courting your lady?"

"She invited me for supper," he admitted.

"Then go ready yourself," she said. "You look like a drowned rat."

She gave him a shove toward the keep and the stairs, and he was off without another word.

"Just don't go gathering flowers to impress her," she called after him.

NINE

"*H*E KISSED ME, Gisela." Clarice paced her friend's small cookshop. "Just like that, and then he asked me to go home with him."

Gisela pushed a strand of flaxen hair back under her mobcap. "And when he comes tonight, what will you tell him?" she asked, her words directed to the table where she was counting the strawberry tarts Clarice had brought her.

"I don't know what to tell him. He cannot have been serious, anyway." Drawing a deep breath, Clarice took the empty basket off her arm and set it on the table. "Watch where you're running, Mary!"

"You as well, Anne," Gisela chided her sprite of a child as she watched the two girls race around the cookshop. "You're making me dizzy." She reached out a plump hand to stop her daughter's hectic progress. "Go into the back and fetch Mrs. Bradford two loaves of bread."

"As you wish, Mama." Laughing, Anne streaked past a lace curtain and into the next room, Mary close on her heels.

Clarice sighed. "I'm still wondering how it is I invited him to supper. I was leaving to go home and dry off, and the words just came out of my mouth, all by themselves."

"All by themselves, is it?" When Clarice kept her lips pressed tight, Gisela leaned closer. "You like him, don't you?"

"He's good to Mary. Patient. He told her a story. And her eyes light up when—"

"This isn't about Mary." With a self-satisfied smile, Gisela counted coins to pay Clarice for the tarts. "It's true your daughter could use a man in her life. Can't we all?" Her kind brown eyes sparkled when she laughed. "But this is about you, Clarice, and what you want for yourself."

"I've been happy alone with Mary. After what I went through with Will, I value my independence."

"And?" The money jingled when Gisela scooped it up.

"He's young."

"How young?"

She bit her lip. "Twenty-four."

"A man grown. If it doesn't bother him, why should

it bother you? Other women will be envious." When Clarice rolled her eyes, Gisela handed her the coins. "And?"

The money clinked in Clarice's hands as she toyed with it, pouring the small pile from one palm to the other. "Scotland. He lives in Scotland. For heaven's sake, I've never even been to London!"

"And?"

She lowered her head, and her voice dropped to a defeated whisper. "My skin tingles when he touches me. I"—she looked up—"I've never felt like this before."

"I felt like that once upon a time." Gisela's words sounded far away, as far away as where she seemed to be staring. "Then Tim succumbed to the smallpox, and here I am...running the cookshop alone. Alone, Clarice." Her gaze focused on her friend. "It isn't good to be alone."

"I have Mary," Clarice said doggedly.

And I'm terrified, she added to herself.

"For how many years will you have her?" Gisela asked. "They grow. They grow and they're gone. You cannot live your life through a child, dearie. That wouldn't be fair to either of you."

TEN

"*D*ELICIOUS." Cameron pushed back from the table. "You're a woman of many talents. I thank you for the fine meal."

Her cheeks burning, Clarice rose to clear the plates. "It was nothing compared to what they serve at the castle."

"I've told you, Clarice, I'm a simple country man. I prefer simple country food."

His words weren't mere flattery—he'd polished off two servings of the stewed venison she'd prepared. She leaned close to access his empty plate. He smelled fresh and faintly spicy, not just the clean scent of the river, but like he'd bathed afterward at the castle, using expensive imported soap. Her husband had worked hard at the mill and rarely bathed—he'd usually smelled of stale sweat.

She jumped back when Cameron released an ear-splitting sneeze. She couldn't help but stare at him. He'd been sneezing ever since he'd arrived.

He shook his head as though to clear it. "Oh, I'll admit that once in a while it's nice to eat fancy. But a man could fall ill eating like that every day, aye?"

"I hope you're not falling ill now," she told him, her heart thudding at the sudden thought. The Black Death had swept through England two years earlier, devastating the population. And its first symptom was sneezing.

His face turned red. "It's just—" Cupping his hands over his mouth, he sneezed again.

Mary stared at him with open admiration. "You have the loudest sneeze I've ever heard."

"Mary!" Clarice admonished, although she'd been thinking the same thing herself before the possibility of serious illness distracted her.

He sneezed yet again, seeming to shake the cottage walls. "My apologies. It's just—" Another explosion had Clarice backing away in an effort avoid this plague.

It was all she could do not to grab her daughter and run for the door.

His eyes filled with regret, he rubbed a finger beneath his nose. "It's just the flowers," he admitted sheepishly.

"The what?" Mary asked, nibbling on a nail while

Clarice wracked her brain, wondering if her daughter had touched him.

"The flowers." He gestured toward the middle of the table, where Clarice had placed a bowl crammed with cheerful posies she'd picked from her garden. "They make me sneeze."

His words finally got through to her. As he drew breath in preparation for another discharge, Clarice snatched up the bowl, clutching it to her chest and sagging with relief. "Flowers make you sneeze?"

With an obvious effort, he held back. "Aye. I've always been that way—I don't know why."

"Lud." And here she'd worried he'd been on the verge of death. Trying not to laugh—at herself or his absurd affliction, or maybe both—she backed toward the door. "Let me just take these outdoors."

Cameron began to rise, as though he intended to help her. Or to leave.

"Mary," she choked out, "will you please pour Sir Cameron more ale?" She hurried outside, closing the door behind her before she slumped against it, attacked by a fit of the giggles like she'd never experienced.

Around this man, she seemed to be a different woman. She had to get herself under control. Biting her tongue, she drew a deep breath and used every ounce of her will to keep a straight face as she reentered the cottage.

As she'd requested, Mary had poured more ale.

Apparently recovered, Cameron sipped and chatted with the girl while Clarice bustled about, calming herself and lighting candles to ward off the dark that was swiftly falling. Though she hadn't a clue whether he would stay a spell longer or not, she was hoping the cozy lit room and another cup of ale would keep him there awhile.

To her vast surprise, she found herself craving another kiss. What could it hurt? A memory to keep her warm at night.

He'd removed his surcoat and sat at her table in a thin lawn shirt, the sleeves rolled up to reveal tanned, muscled forearms. That small display of skin was enough to remind her how he'd looked and felt all wet, with his clothes plastered to his body. Firm and strong, so unlike her husband's aging form. She'd been distracted to the point that she'd nearly forgotten to eat.

Yet he hadn't so much as touched her all evening. She wondered whether he'd given up, or whether he was simply gentleman enough not to press his suit in her daughter's plain sight. She hoped it was the latter.

She was dying for a kiss.

Although the thought of anything more intimate scared the very wits out of her, she found Cameron Leslie's kisses unbearably exciting. But that was because she'd never really been kissed before. A mindless grinding of the lips, yes, but not a real kiss as she'd come to know a kiss this afternoon.

The rest she could happily live without. She knew what *that* felt like, and why anyone would ever call it *making love* was beyond her comprehension. A glossy lie, that, doubtless invented by men to keep virgins from abandoning their marriage beds.

"Well, I've got two choices." Refilled ale cup notwithstanding, Cameron rose. "I can either leave or we can dance."

"Dance?" Whatever was he talking about? Slowly she removed the apron that covered her navy blue dress. A nice dark color. Even if she were soaking wet, he wouldn't be able to see through it.

"Aye, dance," he said. "I was supposed to practice my dancing tonight, in preparation for Friday's ball. Lady Kendra told me in no uncertain terms that I was to return early or dance here instead."

She didn't fall for that story, but when he began pushing the table and chairs out of the way, she couldn't seem to find the words to tell him no. Courtly dancing was for couples, mostly. He would have to touch her.

Her hands tingled at the mere thought.

Mary scraped a chair across the floor. "May I dance, too?"

"Of course you may." He brushed his palms on his plain wool breeches. "We'll start with the minuet. I need the most practice in that—"

"We've got no music," Mary pointed out.

"I can count the beats." He cleared his throat and

launched directly into the lesson. "We count six for each minuet step, but the first movement is only a plié—"

"A what?" Mary cocked her golden head.

"A plié. Just turn out your feet and bend your knees a little."

"Like this?" She pliéd until her bottom nearly touched the floor.

Clarice's heart melted when she saw him bite back a laugh. "Nay, princess. Just a wee bit. Like this." He demonstrated. "Now, that's really naught but a preparation for the step, so we start with the last beat of the previous bar. Six, one, two, three, four, five; six, one, two—"

"I think I feel the headache coming on," Clarice interrupted, putting a hand to her brow. "This is terribly complicated, isn't it?"

"You'll do fine. Follow me. Plié, then step forward with your right foot and rise on your toes. Close in your left foot and lower your heels." As best they could, Clarice and Mary executed the steps while he watched. "Good. Now the same on the other side." Counting off, he danced along. "Six, one, two, three, four, five. Smaller steps, Princess Mary. The steps must be tiny to fit in the beats. Six, one, two, three, four, five…"

When he took Mary's hands to show her how they would dance together, Clarice wanted to scream. Not that she begrudged her daughter the attention, but lud, she'd been waiting all night to touch him. And she felt downright silly dancing alone.

"Six, one, two, three, four, five. La la la, la la la—"

"What are the words?" Mary broke in, stopping midstep.

Cameron blinked. "It doesn't have words." He tugged on Mary's hands to get her dancing again.

"Oh." She stayed stubbornly still and ruminated on that a moment. "I like songs with words."

He shrugged. "I know no words to this one, Princess Mary."

"Then I will sing something else." And without further ado, she launched into a lovely rendition of "The Twenty-Ninth of May."

"Let the bells in steeples ring
And music sweetly play
That loyal Tories mayn't forget
The twenty-ninth of May."

The charming dimples appeared when Cameron grinned. "You sing beautifully, princess." And finally, while Mary's sweet voice trilled the lilting tune, he dropped her hands and took Clarice's.

Mary made her way to a chair.

"Twelve years was he banish'd
From what was his due

And forced to hide in fields and woods
From Presbyterian crew;
But God did preserve him,
As plainly you do see
The blood-hounds did surround the oak
While he was in the tree."

Clarice's feet seemed to glide effortlessly, her body guided by Cameron's warm hands holding hers. Her gaze was locked on his compelling hazel eyes. Her blood pumped much harder than the sedate dance should warrant. Lud, what was happening to her? If her daughter weren't watching, she feared she'd throw herself into his arms.

His intimate smile suggested he just might be reading her mind, and her heart skipped a beat. His hands tightened on hers when she would have stumbled, but he didn't comment on her clumsiness. "She sings of King Charles's restoration, aye?"

"P-pardon?" The song was the farthest thing from her mind.

"I'm speaking of Mary." The dimples winked, telling her he was pleased with her discomposure. "Her song tells of the Restoration, of Charles hiding in the Royal Oak."

"Oh. Yes." Somehow, probably owing to Cameron's skill, her feet kept moving in time to the melody. He must have been jesting when he said he needed practice; he was a superb dancer. "It's a Cavalier ballad she sings. Cainewood—the whole village—was a Royalist strong-hold throughout the Civil War. In support of the marquess, you understand. His family was fiercely Royalist—his parents both died in the Battle of Worcester."

"Do you remember that?"

"Most certainly." Then she remembered something else, and her heart dropped to her knees. "You were too young, weren't you? I'd wager you don't remember the Commonwealth. It was no trial to you, was it, that sad period in our history?"

For a moment, lost in his gaze and the dance, she'd forgotten their age difference. But it would be there, wouldn't it? Always. Different life experiences.

"Nay. I don't remember overmuch," he admitted, confirming her suspicions. "I was but a bairn. And though London holds rule over Scotland, you must remember we are quite far removed from what happens here."

Her voice dropped to a whisper. "We haven't much in common, do we? You're Scottish, I'm English…"

A profound sense of loss swept through her as her words trailed off.

> "So let the bells in steeples ring,
> And music sweetly play,
> That loyal Tories may…n't…forget

The…twen…ty…ninth…"

The song trailed off as well. Curled up on the chair, Mary was sound asleep. Their dance ground to a halt. In unison, they both shot her a glance before their eyes met.

"I want you, Clarice."

She looked down at her scuffed black slippers. No glass shoe, to be sure. "I was never meant to be a lady… indeed, I wouldn't even know how to behave."

With a finger under her chin, he brought her gaze back to his. "Exactly like you do. You're the best woman I've ever met."

Her smile was quick but sad. "And you're the most charming man *I've* ever met."

"Nay, I'm serious." His eyes searched hers. "You've the kindest heart, the sweetest soul. I wouldn't want you to behave any other way than you do already. And no matter what you say, we have quite a bit in common." Cameron's voice went suddenly lower, husky. "Most importantly, what we have in common is this…"

And he pressed his mouth to hers. His hands went to the small of her back, pressing her body to his as well. And heaven help her, she went willingly. Eagerly. Her lips opened beneath his, aching for the sweep of his clever tongue.

When he finally pulled back, she was breathless. Lightheaded.

Halfway in love.

"Now I'll hear no more talk of what we don't have in common," he told her. "What we do have in common is much more pleasant, don't you agree?"

She nodded, then shook her head. "But there are other things—"

"Aye?" His hands gripped her shoulders, and he kissed her again, short and bittersweet. "I will hear of them, then. We will speak of those things tomorrow."

"Tomorrow?"

"Today you fed me, tomorrow I'll feed you." Another kiss. Clearly he meant it to be short, but she kept her mouth fused to his when he would have pulled away, sinking into the caress. With a groan, he capitulated, and for a glorious space of time Clarice was positive there was nothing occupying his mind save for her. The power was heady. When she finally let him release her, she grinned, licking his taste on her lips.

His answering grin was a bit too cocky for her comfort. He dropped his hands from her shoulders and strode to reclaim his surcoat.

"Tomorrow," he repeated, shrugging into it. "A picnic. I will call for you at noon. And Mary, of course. She may bring her friend Anne if it pleases her."

Her gaze shot to her daughter. Lud, she'd been

wantonly kissing a man, and Mary there in the room. Sensible Clarice had lost her senses.

"Don't worry," he said, reading her mind. "She saw nothing."

On his way to the door, he paused to draw her close and plant one more kiss that left her reeling. He was outside and down her garden path before she could catch her breath. A final sneeze drifted back to her.

Noon. Fifteen hours from now. Fifteen hours until she would have to tell him the one thing that would send him running from her as fast as his legs would carry him.

This had gone much too far already.

ELEVEN

"HERE'S A BONNIE loch near Leslie."
Seated on the blanket he'd brought—which
he'd positioned as far from any flowers as possible—
Cameron crossed his arms behind his head and leaned
back against the trunk of a tree. "But not nearly as large
as this one."

Clarice smiled, watching Mary play with her friend
Anne by the lake's edge. "We are fortunate the marquess
allows us to enjoy his park."

Indeed, this patch of England was a sylvan scene,
blue water lapping softly at green shores. Friendly
swans roamed the gently sloped grassy banks, begging
crumbs from the picnickers who sat shaded beneath the
tall, leafy trees.

Before they'd eaten, the girls had begged dancing

lessons from Cameron. Right there in the open, he'd taught them all a branle, the courante, an almain, and the English pavane. "Lady Kendra's been busy," he'd told Clarice.

Now, watching her lick the delicious stickiness of roast chicken from her hands made him envy her lucky fingers. She turned to the huge picnic basket he'd brought with him from the castle. "Lud, there's enough food left to satisfy the entire village."

He grinned. "I told Cook I needed to feed four ravenous folk."

Sipping wine from a pewter goblet, she sent him a mock glare over the rim. "Are you telling me you didn't prepare all this yourself?"

"Nay." Cameron crossed his long legs. "I suppose you should know I cannot cook. That's why I require a wife."

Though he'd said it in jest, he was pleased to see she didn't flinch at his words. Maybe she was getting used to the idea.

Tomorrow was the ball, and Sunday he'd be leaving for home.

The realization hit with a stab of desperation. He couldn't leave her here. Whatever bond he'd felt upon meeting her, since then it had grown. He was more than certain of his feelings now.

Aye, he'd known her but a few days. Aye, it was

daft. But he'd always been a man who knew what he wanted, and what he wanted was Clarice.

He suddenly reached to pull her to him, to hold her close, to devour her sweet mouth, to convince her, once and for all, that she didn't want to live without him any more than he did without her.

Her goblet fell to the ground and rolled down the mild slope. With her palms flat on his chest, she pushed away and sat straight. "I cannot do this." Her words came in a harsh whisper. "I'm feeling too close, and… you're leaving."

She shot a glance to where Mary played by the water, oblivious.

"Clarice." Fingers on her chin, he gently eased her gaze back to his. "Lord knows I've tried to be patient, but I want you. If you didn't believe it before, maybe you will now. You have to now, or it will be too late." He studied her eyes, the gray bright with a sheen of tears. "Do you truly think it matters that you've years to your credit I haven't lived?"

"No," she whispered, for all the world looking defeated. "It's—"

"You cannot believe you don't deserve a baronet. For heaven's sake, all that means is I own some land. And with it comes a title of sorts. But I'm not nobility, Clarice, and even if I were, I'd still want you."

"I know."

Then why did she look like her heart would break?

"Would you be so unhappy, then, to leave the place of your birth?"

"No." She shook her head vehemently. "That's not...no."

"Are you afraid, then, to come away with me unwed? Afraid for your soul? For though the kirk may say it's wrong, the truth is I cannot wait three weeks for banns to be called. I must get home. And the thought of leaving you here…"

"No…that's not the problem, either. I cannot marry you, Cameron. I cannot. It wouldn't be fair to you, can you not see that? I'm not young anymore, and—"

"I told you, I care not about such things!"

"Let me finish—"

"A handfasting, then—"

"A what?" She blinked, clearly confused.

"A handfasting. At home, we don't have too many clergymen, as you do here. And so it is custom to join hands, and to pledge to each other to live as man and wife for a year and a day. At the end of that time, if no child is conceived, the couple can choose to part ways. When next a priest comes to visit, the marriage is confirmed in the eyes of the kirk. It's simple, aye?"

"It's impossible," she whispered.

He didn't understand. "Why would you think so? It's the perfect solution. A time-honored ritual…tell me true, would you feel unwed if the ceremony weren't performed by a member of the clergy?"

She shook her head. "I was wed during the Commonwealth." Cameron knew that during Cromwell's rule, marriage had been a civil matter only, not considered to be any business of God's. "And truly wed I was," she added, visibly shuddering. "It took no clergyman to bind me to Will."

Once again he wondered what this marriage of hers had been like. But this was not the time to probe.

"Then what is your objection, if I may ask? I know you like me—no, more than that. And I won't hear otherwise."

"Whenever my husband…" Her voice dropped to a whisper, then faded away entirely.

"Aye?"

"I cannot be a true wife to any man," she blurted all of a sudden. "I was married fourteen years. Long years. Yet I never once enjoyed sharing a bed with my husband. He said I was…frigid." Her face turned red, but she held Cam's gaze. "I hate that word. But it fits. When it comes to intimacy, I feel…nothing. Nothing but pain and revulsion and fear."

Cameron drew a deep breath and let it out. "That was with him. You don't feel revulsion and fear when I kiss you," he pointed out carefully.

"That's different. I had never been kissed before—" His mouth gaped open, and she held up a hand. "Not really. Not what, with you, I've come to know as a kiss. It was new to me, and yes, wonderful. But I know what the other is like. I don't know how other women stand it. I know only that, for me, it can never be something I more than tolerate. Barely."

He knew she was wrong. But he also knew that no words would convince her of that. "It's sorry I am for you, Clarice. That must have been hard on your marriage."

"It was. Will always said that a night in my bed was...akin to rape. And truth be told, what he did was not all that different from what that other man attempted this summer." A single tear overflowed and traced a path down her cheek. "Will never let me forget, for one minute, what a failure I am as a woman."

"Clarice..."

"That's why I was so thrilled to be given Mary." Her gaze strayed to where her daughter chased Anne along the shore, their giggles floating to them on the breeze. "To have a child, at last, and without having to remarry. I...I don't know if I can go through that again."

A strangled sound escaped his throat, and she looked back to him, her features etched with both pain and determination. "You're young, Cameron Leslie. You have love in your heart, and land and a title to bequeath to children of your body. You shouldn't have to rape your wife in order to get them."

How many times had he pictured those bairns she spoke of running around his castle, growing, working with him side by side? He wanted her for their mother. "Would you be willing to try, Clarice?"

She shrugged. "I tried a thousand times, with all my heart. I always hoped that if I tried, he wouldn't hit me." More tears ran down her cheeks, and he reached to brush them away, feeling a stab of hurt when she pulled back to avoid his hand. "It never worked, and—though I might try again—it never will. Other women speak of a mindless joy, a special bonding. I won't deprive you of that, not even to secure my own happiness. I'm not that selfish. You deserve better."

He knew she was wrong—she was warm, not cold, and, with patience, the right man could overcome the emotional scars of mistreatment.

She was wrong.

But what if *he* were wrong, instead? What if she knew of what she spoke?

Could he live with that?

She rose to her knees, reaching for the goblet that had rolled away, tossing everything back in the basket. "I want you to leave, Cameron."

"What?" Would she cut out his heart?

"I want you to leave." She shoved the basket into his hands, then tossed the blanket over it. "Now. Just leave me alone, like you should have in the first place."

He stared at her for a long moment, until she scrambled to her feet and turned her back.

He slowly stood.

"I love you," he said.

Her shoulders remained stiff, unyielding. The words vibrated across the chasm that stretched between them.

A chasm it seemed he couldn't leap. But he would find a way.

TWELVE

FOR THE FIRST time in close to a week, Clarice felt she'd done a full day's work. She'd made more strawberry tarts and delivered them to Gisela at the cookshop. Her fingers were stained red from picking berries for tomorrow's batch. She'd finished one crewelwork throw and started another, both of which would fetch a tidy sum. The house was swept, the linens washed.

Her heart was empty.

She'd known all along that Cameron wouldn't choose to marry a cold woman. She'd been foolish to allow herself to get close. But though she'd said from the start that she and Mary were better off on their own —and truly meant it as well—the thought of never seeing him again left her feeling like there was a gaping hole in her middle.

Yet surely she would get over that. It was all for the better. She was terrified at what the marriage bed would entail, and having escaped that once, she'd be foolish to go back. She might have lived a fairytale for a week, but she wasn't meant to live in a castle forever.

She was setting supper on the table when the rattle of carriage wheels began parading down her street. One after the other, the local gentry were making their way to the castle for the marquess's wedding celebration ball.

Mary ran to fling open the door. "Look, Mama! Oh, look at the beautiful coaches! Look, that one has four white horses! And I can see inside. That lady's hair has jewels stuck in it!"

"How lovely," Clarice answered with as much enthusiasm as she could muster—which wasn't much. Though she'd never expected to attend the ball—unlike her daughter, never even dreamed of such a thing—that didn't mean she wanted to ogle the guests. She'd prefer to block the entire event from her mind. Just knowing Cameron was there, probably already dancing the new dances, made her heart ache anew.

"Eleven carriages so far, Mama."

"Is that so?" Clarice struggled to pull herself together. "How many if three more arrive?" she forced herself to ask, playing their old game. "How many then?"

Mary's golden head tilted, but she stayed facing

away, her gaze glued to the proceedings outdoors. "Fourteen," she finally announced, pride in her small voice. "Fourteen, is that right? And here come three more now."

She yawned, covering her mouth with one small hand; Clarice had kept her busy all the day long, running, fetching, and helping wherever a girl her size could help. Then suddenly she stilled, and her voice sounded puzzled. "Here comes one from the other direction, Mama. Do you s'pose the party is full?"

"I think not."

"But the carriage is stopping, Mama. It's not turning around. The party must be too full."

Despite her melancholy, Clarice found herself laughing. "I imagine the ballroom is large enough to accommodate half the population of Sussex."

"Cainewood doesn't boast a proper ballroom," came a deep voice, "but they're using the great hall. And your mama's right—the chamber is unlikely to be strained to the bursting anytime soon."

"Cameron?" Clarice whispered.

"Good eve, princess." He swung Mary up into his arms and stepped inside, dressed in the blue velvet suit he had worn to the wedding.

Lud, he was devastating.

Wickedly confident, his grin lit up a place in Clarice's heart. But she steeled herself to caution. "Good evening, Sir Cameron."

"Clarice." He nodded, a gallant incline of his head. "I hope you remember the new dances."

"Wh-what?"

"The new dances. I'll be wanting to dance with you at the ball."

Whatever could he be talking about? "I'm not going to the ball!"

"Oh, aye, you are. And it's started already, so we'd best be on our way." Setting Mary on her feet, he brushed a stray blond curl from her face. "You'll be needing a ribbon for your hair, princess, and you must put on your best gown."

Mary's eyes were round as two blue saucers. "Am I going to the ball, too?"

"Not exactly. But you can watch from the minstrel's gallery." The minstrel's gallery. The exact place Clarice had wished she could watch from a few days earlier. "And there will be one special ceremony where I'm hoping you'll want to bear witness."

"What about a bear?"

"Bear witness. You'll see. Then, when you get tired, you may sleep in the nursery."

"With baby Jewel?"

"The very same. And her nurse to watch over you both."

"You've planned everything," Clarice put in, finally finding her tongue. "But I'll thank you not to make promises to my daughter that you cannot keep. I cannot go to the ball. I'm no lady, and I've nothing to wear."

"Did you think I taught you those dances only so you could do them with Mary?" The ostrich plume on Cameron's hat bobbed when he shook his well-groomed head. "I've a gown for you in the carriage—just wait here while I fetch it."

"Wait here," Clarice scoffed, turning to ladle her soup. "As though I've anywhere to go. Certainly not to a ball at the castle."

But a moment later he was back, a brilliant yellow gown over one arm that reminded her of the buttercups alongside the River Caine. It had an underskirt of golden tissue, and a wide gold flounce all the way around the bottom.

"I had the seamstress add the flounce," Cameron explained, "since you're a wee bit taller than Kendra."

An understatement if ever she'd heard one. But her fingers itched to touch the sumptuous fabric. "You expect me to…wear this?"

"Aye. I went to great trouble to have it readied when both Lady Cainewood and Lady Kendra were wanting their new gowns finished at the same time. And…" From his surcoat pocket, he pulled a short strand of large, lustrous pearls. "I want you to wear this, too."

She'd never seen anything quite so beautiful. "But nothing has changed," she said as he stepped behind her to fasten the clasp. The pearls felt heavy against her collarbones. "Between us, or otherwise."

When he came around to face her, his eyes were as earnest as ever. "I didn't think anything had changed. I want to take you to the ball, Clarice." He held out a golden stomacher that matched the dress. "Hurry. It's already started."

Mary snatched it from his hands and shoved it at her mother. "Yes, hurry, Mama. We must bank the fire, lest the soup burn. Will we eat supper at the ball?"

"Aye, delicacies like you've never tasted. Your mama and I will bring a plate to the nursery for you."

Mary clapped her hands. "Hurry, Mama!" she repeated. She started working the laces on the front of her dress.

"I'll wait for you in the carriage," Cameron said over his shoulder as he headed out the door. "Impatiently."

THIRTEEN

"*I* FEEL LIKE I'm in a dream," Clarice said an hour later. "Dancing at a ball in the castle. Ever since the day I met you, I've felt like I'm in a dream. A fairytale."

Cameron twirled her into the next step. "The dream can last forever, Clarice, if only you'll say aye."

"Oh, Cam…" Tonight, if she had any say in the matter, reality wouldn't intrude. There would be time for sorrow and regret tomorrow. "If only things could be different. I cannot be a real wife to you—not the kind of wife you deserve—"

"What I deserve is for me to decide, for me to choose. And I choose you. What you speak of is only one small part of marriage. The other parts are much more important. I choose you, Clarice. I choose you and Mary."

She watched his gaze stray up to the minstrel's gallery, where her daughter's small face appeared between the slats. He released Clarice long enough to wave, then grinned when Mary waved back.

"You said you were willing to try." They rose on their toes, then moved closer together. "But even without that, what you are is enough for me."

And right there, in the great hall in front of all the glittering aristocrats, he stopped and leaned to give plain Clarice Bradford a kiss.

"Since you're the practical sort," he continued when he resumed the dance, "I shall give you my practical arguments. I've no wish to marry for lust. That often fades anyway, or so I've been told. I wish to marry for love, for companionship, for the helpmate I know you will be." He drew a breath that she might have thought was shaky, if she didn't know him better. "But mostly because I cannot live without you. Since the moment I laid eyes on you, I've known you were meant to be mine. Just as you are, Clarice. I won't be expecting you to change."

"I wish I could believe you," she whispered.

"What's stopping you?" he demanded, displaying the quick temper she'd spotted briefly the day they went boating and again at the picnic. She had to remind herself she'd seen nothing in him to lead her to believe he might hurt her. "What cause have I given you to doubt my word? Ever?"

"None," she said honestly. "But you walked away. When I told you I am...fr-frigid"—she stumbled over the word—"you walked away."

"You *told* me to walk away."

The look on his face sparked her guilt. At the time, she'd been certain permission to leave was what he wanted. But now she wasn't so sure.

"Regardless," he said, "it's sorry I am that I did walk away." His hazel eyes looked so earnest, she couldn't doubt him. "I needed to think it through; I'll admit to that, Clarice. In that very moment I wasn't certain of my feelings. But now I know my heart. I've told you the truth, and I've never lied to you before, so I'll thank you not to accuse me of it now." His hands squeezed hers. "What you have to offer is enough. I cannot live without you—not happily, at least."

All at once, rather than seeming too young, he seemed wise beyond his years. And Clarice felt young and untried, frightened of the future yet even more afraid to refuse her one chance at happiness.

"What do you say?" Cameron stopped, right there in the middle of the dance. "Will you become my hand-fasted wife, Clarice Bradford? Tonight? For day after tomorrow I leave for my castle, and I'll be wanting to take you with me. You and Mary."

"She'll think she's a princess."

"Nothing will make me happier than she be *my* princess. Except, of course, if you'll be my wife. Lady

Leslie. It has a nice ring to it, aye?" His smile made her heart turn over. "The glass shoe fits you, Clarice. You deserve to wear it."

"The glass shoe would never fit." She glanced down at the hem of the gorgeous gown, thankful it was plenty long to hide her plain black slippers. He hadn't thought to bring her proper dress shoes, and for that he'd apologized profusely, though she suspected he'd wanted to but hadn't been able to find ones that fit her big feet.

Not that she'd have chosen to wear formal shoes, anyway. She could barely perform the new dances in flat shoes, let alone heels.

"It fits," he insisted.

It still sounded impossible. She'd be living in a castle. Dazed, she glanced around Cainewood's enormous great hall: the polished plank floor, the tapestries on the walls, the intricate oak hammerbeam ceiling. The chamber exuded a stately majesty she could never aspire to live up to.

"Leslie Castle is nothing like this," Cameron said, reading her mind as only he could. "Nothing. It isn't ancient like this, but nearly new—Caithren's father built it. It boasts naught but fifteen rooms, small rooms, none of them anything like the massive chambers here. It's but a fortified house, really, built to look like a castle."

"Fifteen rooms," she murmured. "*Naught* but fifteen rooms." Her lips curved in a wry smile. "I've only ever lived in one."

"Don't worry—I will hire someone to clean it for you. You won't be expected to break your back making our castle a home."

"That wasn't what I was thinking." Good heavens, she would have a servant? Whoever would have thought it?

But of course she would. She would be Lady Leslie.

"Will you marry me, Clarice? Please. Tonight. Right now." Dropping one of her hands, he pulled a white ribbon from his surcoat pocket. "Mary is waiting for your answer."

"Mary?" She glanced up to the gallery, and her daughter waved again. "Mary knows you wish to do this tonight?"

"Well, now, while we were waiting for you in the carriage, she asked again about the bear. She was afraid it might be dangerous." He grinned, displaying the dimples that reminded her he was young. But wise, she reminded herself. So very wise. And entirely too charming. "So I explained to her about bearing witness, and what a very important job that would be. She assured me she is mature enough to handle it."

"Oh," she said, her free hand rising to trace the curve of the unfamiliar pearls around her neck. She felt overwhelmed, pressured from all sides. And within herself. She'd been so sure she wanted to be free of men, just she and Mary making a life for themselves. But Cameron would leave on Sunday, and she knew if he left alone, he'd be taking her heart along with him.

She closed her eyes and drew a deep breath, uncertain of her answer until she opened them. Then, "Yes," she whispered. "I will be honored to become handfasted to you, Cameron Leslie. Tonight."

He let out a whoop that had heads turning as he pulled her from the great hall.

Laughing, she ran after him, and his cousin, Lady Cainewood, came running after them both.

"Cameron! What are you up to?"

He stopped in the entry, a three-story stone chamber graced with impossibly tall columns and a magnificent staircase. "Getting handfasted, cousin. Right now."

"Without asking me to attend? How dare you?" His cousin's words sounded stern, but her hazel eyes, so like his, were dancing conspiratorially. "Where? I must fetch Jason."

"Not Lord Cainewood," Clarice begged under her breath. "I couldn't…"

"You alone, Cait." Cameron started up the steps. "Mary will be the second witness."

Without hesitation, Lady Cainewood followed. When they reached the top of the stairs, Mary came running down the corridor and threw herself into Cameron's arms. "Did she say yes?"

"Aye, princess, she did. Aren't we lucky?"

"Can I call you Papa?"

He froze in his tracks, clearly made breathless with surprise. "I would be honored," he told Mary gravely, his voice husky with emotion.

And in that moment, Clarice knew for certain she had made the right choice, no matter how frightened she was of the marriage bed, and moving to Scotland, and becoming a lady. It was the right choice for her daughter, and Mary was more important than all the mental obstacles barring Clarice's way.

He led them all to a chamber and threw open the door. Clarice's breath caught in wonder.

The entire room seemed golden. A carved bedstead was gilded and hung with golden brocade. The rest of the furniture was upholstered and gilded to match. The largest mirror Clarice had ever seen hung over a marble-topped table. She glimpsed herself in it, looking flushed and awed and younger even than Cameron.

"The Gold Chamber," Lady Cainewood explained. "My husband told me it's saved for honored guests, and no guest here is more important than Cameron."

Cameron rolled his eyes. "It's the truth I've felt rather ridiculous bumping about this enormous room by myself." He took Clarice's hand and pulled her inside. "It will be much nicer in here tonight with you by my side."

"Me? In here?" She couldn't imagine. She was afraid to even stand on the patterned carpet that covered the floor. Her mind boggled at the luxury and expense.

"Did you think I'd be spending our wedding night alone? Or in your little cottage? Not that it isn't nice," he rushed to add. "You keep it quite bonnie. But it's one room, you see, and with Mary—"

"We all see," his cousin put in. "And you are more than welcome to stay here, Mrs. Bradford, until the day you leave for Leslie."

Clarice wasn't at all sure she was mentally prepared for a wedding night. "I wouldn't presume, Lady Cainewood—"

"You must call me Caithren. Or Cait, if you please. We're about to be cousins, after all."

Could this get any more unbelievable?

"Now," Cameron said, "take my hands, right to right, and left to left. In this way our arms make the symbol of infinity, signifying our commitment to be together. Forever."

It sounded too much, too soon. "I thought you said it was for a year and a day?"

"Normally, aye. But for us, forever."

When he looked at her like that, she was hard put to refuse him anything. She only hoped this strange ceremony included a kiss at the end like the traditional one, because she was dying to feel his mouth on hers. No matter that her daughter and his cousin were watching.

He dropped one of her hands long enough to give the ribbon to Mary. "Can you tie this around our four hands, princess?"

"I'll do it," Caithren volunteered.

"No, I can do it." Proudly Mary stepped up and took the white ribbon. "I learned how to tie last year, didn't I, Mama?"

"You surely did, poppet."

Cam reclaimed Clarice's hand. "Then tie it well, princess, for it symbolizes how tightly our family will be bound together. You, me, and your mama."

"Wait." Frowning, Mary chewed on a nail. "At Lady Cainewood's wedding…well, shouldn't Mama be holding flowers?"

"Nay!" Cam and Cait shouted together. Eyes wide, Mary jumped, and in spite of the serious occasion, Clarice found herself laughing.

What a marvelous new life she was going to have.

She sobered when Mary came closer, and if the bow was a bit crooked when she finished tying, it didn't matter. "Perfect," Cameron declared.

Then he dropped to one knee and captured Clarice's gaze with his.

"I present to you, Clarice, my love and my pledge. May I never knowingly or willingly do anything to harm nor grieve you in any fashion. Accept this pledge as a token of my trust. Like our hands are bound, may our love be as strong. That which is mine is yours, my heart and all my worldly belongings. Will you share my life with me, Clarice?"

A hush settled over the room, and his hands squeezed hers.

"What am I supposed to say?" she whispered.

"Say aye, my love. Only aye."

She ventured a tremulous smile. "Aye, then. I will share your life. For a year and a day and forevermore."

He rose and leaned forward, his mouth meeting hers in a rush of heat, their bound hands crushed between their bodies.

All too soon, he pulled away.

"Now, Mary," he said huskily. "Cait? Will you untie us, if you please, and bind Mary's hands to ours as well?"

Tears flooded Clarice's eyes as his cousin did as he bid. Soon they were tied together, the three of them, and Cam dropped to one knee again.

"We are bound to you, Mary, from this day forward, as your parents in our hearts and our souls. You have our love, and with it our promise never to harm or grieve you willingly in any fashion. Like our hands are bound, let our love be as strong. Will you share your life with us, and be known from this day forward as Mary Leslie, daughter of Cameron and Clarice?"

"What am *I* s'posed to say?" Mary whispered.

Beneath the ribbon bow, Clarice squeezed her daughter's hand. "Just say yes, sweet."

"Yes!" An exclamation of pure joy, the single word echoed in the ancient stone chamber.

And though Clarice had felt like Mary was hers from the day Lord Cainewood brought the girl to her doorstep, in that moment she felt closer to her daughter than she'd ever thought possible. Bound, as Cameron had said, heart and soul. She would never be able to thank him for this precious gift of belonging.

All at once, Caithren was untying the ribbon, and Cameron raised Mary into the air and gave her resounding kisses on both cheeks. Then he handed her to Clarice, wrapping his arms around them both as though he could protect them from the world.

She hoped he could. She was counting on it.

"Am I a princess now?" Mary asked when he finally released them.

"No, poppet," Clarice started.

"Aye," Cam interrupted before she could say another word. "You're *my* princess. And you always will be, even after you go off and get married."

"I'm never getting married," Mary declared. "I'm going to live with you forever."

Cameron ruffled her golden curls. "Well, now, it's the truth that nothing would make me happier. But we'll have to wait and see what happens, aye? Don't forget that only last week your own mama was saying she'd never get married, either."

"I must get back to the ball." Caithren sighed, then brightened. "I cannot wait to tell everyone the news."

"Nay." Cameron put a hand on her arm. "This is

your night. Yours and Jason's. If you've no objection, I've a mind to take my two women here downstairs for a dance or a dozen—"

"Me, too?" Mary squealed. "Is that why you taught us the dances?"

"Absolutely. We've much to celebrate, the three of us. But in secret, aye? No one else will know it's not only cousin Caithren's wedding we're celebrating, but our wedding-for-three as well. So lock your lips, aye?"

Mary clapped both hands over her mouth and nodded.

"Good." He took her by the hand and Clarice with his other. "Then let us celebrate."

FOURTEEN

*C*ELEBRATE THEY did, dancing the new dances and supping on scrumptious delicacies until the wee hours when the ball finally wound down. The locals headed for home, and guests who'd traveled a distance were each shown to one of Cainewood Castle's hundred chambers. Mary fell asleep on the way up the stairs, and they took her to the nursery and tucked her into one of the small beds that flanked baby Jewel's cradle.

"She looks like a princess," Cameron whispered.

Clarice went on her toes to kiss him on the cheek. "Thank you so much for including her in the handfasting. It meant so much to her." She hesitated a moment, still shy with this man—her new husband. "To both of us."

"To all three of us," he corrected her. He bent to kiss

Mary's little forehead. "Now we've celebrated that, it's time for a more private celebration."

Though she told herself she was being ridiculous, Clarice trembled as they walked the short distance to the Gold Chamber. Once more she was awed by the gorgeous room, though Cam didn't give her much time to admire it. The door had barely shut behind them when he set down the candle he'd been carrying and dragged her up against him and into his arms.

His lips on hers were soft, caressing, almost sweet, but she sensed an urgency in him just before the kiss went hot and fervent. He kissed her senseless, plundering her mouth until she was breathless and tingling all over.

"I'll make you forget them," he promised when he finally pulled away. "Your first husband and the other man who mistreated you."

"I've forgotten them already," she whispered.

"That's not yet true," he said, "but I'll make it true." He lavished her face with little kisses, and her forehead and her neck and her ears. All the while he worked his arms out of his surcoat, and it dropped to the floor with a soft rustle.

Slowly he backed her up, until Clarice felt her legs against the bed. Someone had removed the costly brocade counterpane, and the quilts were folded back in a way she imagined was supposed to be inviting, but only served to boost her anxiety.

When he eased her down to the sheets, her trembling increased. Best to get this over with. She squeezed her eyes shut tight and drew a deep, shuddering breath. "All right," she forced between gritted teeth. "You can do it now."

She waited a few heartbeats, and when he didn't touch her, she opened her eyes. Cameron stood by the bed, staring down at her, his face an inscrutable mask.

She swallowed hard and frowned at him. "Do you not want to do it?"

"You can bet I do." His long fingers worked at the knot in his cravat. "But not until you're ready."

She bit her lip. "I'm ready now. Just…just do it."

"Nay." He drew off the cravat and set it on the bedside table. "I'll know when you're ready. You needn't announce it. Especially when it's not true."

"I'm ready," she insisted, wanting nothing more than to have this part out of the way. This part wasn't a fairytale, and she wanted to get back to the fairytale part of her exciting new life.

Tomorrow she and Mary would pack up their things and say goodbye to Gisela and Anne and all their other friends and neighbors. Then Sunday they'd be on their way to live in a castle…

"You're not ready," Cameron disagreed with staid calmness. His gaze was steady, his voice tender and huskily seductive. "When your breath comes heavy, when you ache deep inside, when your body trembles with need, not fear…*then* you'll be ready. And I won't be *doing it* until I know you want it just as much as I do."

"Oh, Cam." Her heart ached at the thought of disappointing him, but she didn't think that was the ache deep inside he was talking about. "I thought I'd explained this to you—I thought you understood. I'll never want it as much as you do. I'll never want it at all."

"Then we won't do it," he said simply.

Her jaw went slack, and a moment passed before her tongue could form any words. "You—you cannot mean that," she finally stammered.

"I don't lie, Clarice."

"But never…" It was incomprehensible. "Do you mean to say that if I don't want it, you will never do it at all?"

"Aye."

She struggled up on her elbows to better see into his eyes. He truly looked sincere. And he'd never given her cause to distrust him. She felt a flood of relief, mixed with wonder and a rush of love. "Thank you," she whispered.

Facing away, he sat on the edge of the bed and pulled off one of his shoes. "I don't think it will come down to never, though," he said conversationally. "I reckon that not too long from now you'll be dying to have me inside you."

She blushed at the frank talk. "Maybe," she said doubtfully, not wanting to argue. "In a few years."

"I was thinking more like a few hours." His second shoe hit the floor, and he shifted on the bed to look at her. "Or minutes."

Her elbows slid out from under her, and she lay flat, staring up at him. His eyes darkened. Thinking of the way he talked—*when your breath comes heavy, when you ache deep inside, when your body is trembling...you'll be dying to have me inside you*—made the heat rush to her cheeks and her mouth go dry.

She licked her lips. No man had ever talked to her like that. In fact, her first husband had never talked in bed at all—he'd either yelled or taken his pleasure as quickly as he could, in sullen silence.

When Cameron began to lower his mouth to meet hers, a little whimper rose from her throat. She wasn't quite sure whether it was a sign of fear or anticipation.

"Hush," he soothed, and sat up. In a businesslike way, he slipped his hands behind her neck and unclasped the pearls. They glistened in the candlelight as he slowly laid them on the bedside table with a series of soft clicks. "Do you like your wedding present?" he asked.

"Pardon?"

He was already removing her shoes. "Your wedding present. The pearls."

She gasped, and it wasn't only because his hands

were streaking under her skirts. "But…when? How? I thought they were borrowed. It's too much—"

"Don't be silly, Clarice," he said, plucking off a garter. "Lady Leslie should own a nice set of pearls." The second garter joined the first on the floor. "Did you know your new cousin Amy is a jeweler?"

"Amy? Oh, you mean Lady Greystone? Yes. She gave Mary a locket for Christmas."

"Well, she asked a mere pittance for those pearls. Having a jeweler in the family proves to be mighty convenient."

The thought of lords and ladies as family made her head spin. Or maybe it was his hands slowly rolling her stockings down and off, his fingers tracing delicate paths on her legs. He ran a fingertip along the bottom of one bare foot. It made her toes curl and her breath catch.

Supporting himself on his forearms, he moved over her with a gentle smile. "I promise I won't do anything you don't like."

He smelled divinely male, and he felt warm, and because she believed him, his weight on her was more comforting than frightening. "Anything?"

"Anything. For now, I'll just kiss you." He cradled her cheek with a hand and skimmed his thumb over her lips. "You like kissing, aye?"

"Aye," she breathed. "I mean, yes. Kiss me. Please."

When his mouth claimed hers, she let herself slide

into the gentle caress. She trusted him, and he'd said he wouldn't do anything she didn't like.

She definitely liked his kisses.

She still wondered that a man's mouth could be so soft. And when it turned harder, more demanding, she liked that, too. He tasted spicy and sweet, like the wine that had flowed freely at the ball. He nibbled her lips and traced them with his tongue before delving inside to make her mouth burn with fire. When at last he lifted his head, she found herself gasping for air.

Like he'd predicted, her breath was coming heavy.

His lips trailed down to press a soft kiss in the hollow of her neck. "Do you like this, my love?"

"Oh, yes." It was a wonder that a kiss, not even on the mouth, could feel so good. It made her all shivery. Her breathing wasn't getting any calmer.

Between their bodies, his fingers moved to detach the golden stomacher. Beneath it her breasts were laced tightly into the gown's bodice, and he went to work on the bow at the top, then tugged at the laces, and all the while his mouth continued the sensual assault on her sensitive throat.

At last he managed to pull the lacing free. He raised himself and spread the bodice wide, then traced a path with his lips to explore the mounds of her breasts through her flimsy chemise.

"So lovely," he murmured, and his words felt warm through the thin fabric. Clarice's heart skittered, then raced faster, so fast she wondered if he could hear it over the ragged sound of her uncontrolled breathing. He hooked a finger in the chemise's lacy neckline and dragged the material down, fastening his mouth on one rosy peak.

Hot. It felt hot and wet and wickedly wonderful. "Do you like this?" he whispered, his breath ruffling over her sensitized flesh.

In answer, she threaded her hands in his hair and pulled him even closer. Never had she dreamed her breasts would swell and crave a man's touch, a man's lips. Breasts were made to nourish babies, so she hadn't found any use for hers. Until now. Swirling his tongue across her tingling skin, he made his way to her other nipple, suckling it until it puckered in response.

It made her ache deep inside. Like he'd said it would.

When he drew off the gown and chemise, she liked it. When his fingers traced feathery trails all over her body, she liked that, too. When he removed his own clothes, she was surprised to find she liked that very much.

Her hands explored his heated skin, the unfamiliar contours of his muscles, the smooth planes of his back. She'd never voluntarily touched a man before, and touching him gave rise to new feelings, until her body trembled, but not with fear. With need, then, as he'd said it would. She felt like she wanted, yes, *needed* more from him.

Lud, it was just like he'd said it would be.

"I'm ready," she whispered, then drew a sharp breath, shocked that the words had escaped her lips. Surely she couldn't have meant them, couldn't really want him inside her. She knew what that felt like—it hurt. It would ruin all these new and wondrous sensations.

He stilled and rolled to her side. Lifting her hand from where it clenched his shoulder, he brushed his lips over the knuckles. Dark, unfathomable, magnetic, his gaze held hers. "Nay, you're not ready. But you will be, love."

Relief and disappointment mingled, along with anticipation. Her eyes slid closed when he slipped a hand between her legs and urged them apart. His fingers danced on the delicate flesh of her inner thighs, tantalizing, teasing, and her skin tingled almost unbearably.

"Do you like this?" he asked, and she could only nod her response. "Only what you like, Clarice. I promise."

When his hand brushed higher, she nearly leapt off the bed.

"Hush," he murmured in a soothing tone, taking her mouth in a deep kiss. When she relaxed, he raised his head. "A test, love, to see if you like it. Will you trust me?"

She bit her lip and nodded. Slowly he cupped her with a hand. Drawing a deep breath, she nodded again.

And his hand moved.

Lud, what sweet torture. Teasingly seductive, his fingers felt exquisite. "I like it," she whispered.

With an ease she never would have imagined, he slipped a finger inside, and a gasp escaped her lips. Half shock, half incredible pleasure.

Will had never touched her with his hands, only with his fists.

Aroused nearly beyond bearing, Cam struggled to hold himself in check. Sweet Lord, she was tight. And frightened out of her wits, he was sure. Once more he was gripped with a fierce urge to murder her late husband. But she gave off other signals as well, signals that made his heart swell with hope and tenderness.

She felt like heaven in his embrace. Her body exuded a heady, musky scent of arousal that drove his own desire to a fever pitch. When he moved his hand, she responded with a blissful sigh that touched a tender place in his soul. Her hips began to shift, her sighs coming between broken breaths as he continued to caress her, driving them both to the brink.

"I'm ready," she breathed in a velvet-edged whisper.

"Aye, you're ready." He moved over her, settling himself into the cradle of her thighs. Poised to enter her, he gritted his teeth and paused. "Are you sure, my love?"

Her answer was a simple "Yes," her voice laced with wonder. Her hands came around his back and hugged tight. And he slid home, finding sweet glory in the feel of her taking him into herself. He held there, savoring her heat, until, with a tiny whimper that set his heart to singing, she arched under him.

This, Clarice thought, was the real fairytale come true. They moved together in perfect harmony, a slow, thrilling cadence that made passion radiate from deep within her.

Making love.

It was the perfect—the only—way to describe it.

Then faster they moved, until she couldn't think at all. Until, in a brilliant burst of fiery sensation, she catapulted out of her old world and into a new one, a world brimming with love and shining promise.

Across the room, the last candle sputtered and died. Pressed against him in the darkness, as close as two people could be, she could feel Cameron's heart beat in a rhythm to match her own. She reached for his face and took it between her hands. His cheeks were slightly rough beneath her fingers, just enough to remind her that, incredible though it seemed, she shared her bed with a living, breathing man.

And it was glorious.

"I love you," she whispered. "I love you for who you are, and who you've magically made me to be."

"It isn't magic, my love. Or if it is," he mused, his

words warm against her lips, making her ache anew for his kiss, "it's a magic we can only find together." Reading her mind, he fit his mouth to hers in a way that made the heat pool in her middle.

A long, melting time later, he lifted his head. "Together," he repeated.

"Together," she whispered back. Never had she imagined that word would apply to her and a man. But from this moment forward, it did.

For a year and a day and forevermore.

AUTHOR'S NOTE

DEAR READER,

Most of the homes in my books are inspired by real places you can visit. Cainewood Castle is loosely modeled on Arundel Castle in West Sussex. It has been home to the Dukes of Norfolk and their family, the Fitzalan Howards, since 1243, save for a short period during the Civil War. Although the family still resides there, portions of their magnificent home are open to visitors and more than worth a detour, should you ever find yourself in the area.

I hope you enjoyed *If You Dared to Love a Laird*! Next is Kendra's story in *A Duke's Guide to Seducing His Bride*. Please read on for an excerpt.

Always,

Lauren Royal

Read on for an excerpt from

A Duke's *Guide* to Seducing His *Bride*

Book 4 of the
Chase Family Series
by Lauren Royal

Lady Kendra Chase is caught in a compromising embrace with a dashing, mysterious highwayman. Will her brothers really insist she marry him?

Sussex, England
June 1668

KENDRA CHASE adored her brothers, except when she wanted to kill them.

"Jason is right," Ford told her as they rattled down the road in a shabby public coach. "You're twenty-three years old, and it's high time you take a husband."

Kendra slanted a glance at the plainly dressed stranger sharing the coach with them. "Not the Duke of Lechmere," she said with an exasperated glare at her twin. "I won't be 'your graced' for the rest of my life."

Kendra's oldest brother, Jason, tried unsuccessfully to stretch his long legs. "And what, pray tell," he drawled in an annoyed tone, "would be wrong with that? I've never understood what you have against dukes." Crammed onto the bench seat between Kendra and his wife, Caithren, he sighed. "I only wish to see you live a life of comfort. Would you prefer to travel this way all the time?"

As if to drive home her brother's point, the spring-

124 | A DUKE'S GUIDE TO SEDUCING HIS BRIDE EXCERPT

less vehicle lurched in and out of a rut, rattling Kendra's teeth. She gritted them. Though Jason was careful with money, he was, after all, the Marquess of Cainewood, and they did own a rather luxurious carriage. But one of its wheels had broken on their way out of London, and they'd been forced to take public transport—or else risk missing an urgent appointment back home at Cainewood Castle.

An appointment to introduce Kendra to the latest "suitable" man her brothers planned to foist upon her.

"My comfort isn't the issue here—"

"This is your last chance to make your own choice," Jason interrupted her, gathering the cards from the hand of piquet they'd just played. "If you won't marry Lechmere, you'll have to select one of the other men who have offered for you. Or *I* will do the selecting."

"The other men." Kendra tossed her head of dark red curls, not believing her brother's ultimatum for a moment. The wretched day had put him in a bad mood, but he was generally the most reasonable man she knew. "Old but well-off, or widowed and settled with children, or young but just plain *boring*. Stable, wealthy men in the good graces of King Charles, every last one of them."

Jason's green eyes flashed. "Yes, perfectly acceptable, every last one of them."

"As it should be," Ford put in.

Mournfully shaking her head, Kendra sent Caithren an imploring glance. "They'll never understand."

Cait's eyes filled with sympathy and a bit of shared exasperation. She laid a hand on her husband's arm. "I've told you before, Kendra wishes to marry for love, not—"

"Stand and deliver!" a deep voice interrupted from outside.

With an unnerving suddenness, the coach ground to a halt. Stopped in mid-sentence, Cait's mouth gaped, and Kendra's stomach clenched in fear.

Ford leaned forward and pushed open the door. A man on horseback—a highwayman!—poked his head inside.

The most compelling head Kendra had ever seen.

"*You?*" Jason and Ford said together.

They knew this man?

Since Kendra hadn't heard that either of her brothers had been hurt—or even robbed, come to think of it—most of her fear dissipated, and her heart lifted with excitement instead.

Nothing like this had ever happened to her!

Looking slightly disconcerted, the highwayman dismounted. "Aye, it's me," he said slowly. Beneath the mask that concealed the upper half of his face, a grin emerged. An engaging slash of perfect white.

Well, not precisely perfect. One of his front teeth had a small chip, but she found that tiny imperfection endearing. And he was dashing, not to mention forbid-den. If any of her hopeful suitors had been like this man, she'd have married him in a trice.

She wanted to say something to make him notice her. But for the first time in her memory, her mouth refused to work.

His gaze swept the coach's dim interior as though she weren't even there. "You," he said succinctly, motioning to the whey-faced businessman seated beside Ford. "Get out."

"There be five of us in here, three of them men, likely with pistols," the man said stiffly. From his haircut, plain clothes, and the short, boxy jacket beneath his cloak, Kendra knew he was a Puritan. "Perhaps thee had better think again."

"Oh, it's violence you threaten, aye?" The highway-man's voice was deep and a little husky, with, curiously, the barest hint of an accent. "Perhaps *you* had better think again. My friends," he drawled, gesturing toward the hill behind him, "would make certain you cease to exist within the minute. Get out. Now."

Kendra looked out the door and up. Sure enough, there were a dozen or so men at the top of the hill, their guns trained on the coach.

The Puritan must have recognized the threat, for he reluctantly climbed down. Kendra shifted within the coach, the better to see out.

The victim was a good foot shorter than the robber,

who looked impossibly tall and elegant in a jet-black velvet surcoat. Close-faced and resigned, the Puritan emptied his pockets and handed over his money, then turned to reenter the coach.

The highwayman reached to grab the victim's sleeve. "Not so fast."

Visibly shaken, the smaller man stilled but said nothing.

The highwayman shook him a little. "Surely a...man of business, such as yourself, will be carrying more gold on his person than this. Where is it? Sewn into your cloak? Hidden in your luggage?"

Though Kendra could see the rise and fall of his agitated breathing, the Puritan turned back boldly. "Surely *thee* has no need of gold," he spat out, tugging his sleeve from the bigger man's grasp while eyeing his groomed appearance and expensive, tailored suit. "A...*gentleman* such as thyself."

The highwayman's eyes were amber, edged in a deeper hue—bronze, Kendra decided—that now spread in toward the center as his expression hardened. "Your luggage *and* your cloak, then—seeing as you won't cooperate."

He swung his pistol in the coachman's direction. The driver scrambled down and fumbled with the ropes securing the passengers' belongings. A shove sent the Puritan's trunk to the rutted road with a decisive *thunk*.

"Your cloak." The highwayman held out his free

hand, almost as though he were bored, while his victim struggled out of his plain mantle.

"What about *them*?" he sputtered, handing it over. His gaze swung toward the Chases.

The highwayman glanced inside and flashed Kendra's brothers a conspiratorial smile before answering. "They're friends. Good day."

"Good day? *Good day*?" The poor man looked as red as a squalling newborn, and Kendra almost felt sorry for him—until she reminded herself that it was his ilk who had killed her parents during the Civil War.

Her brothers indeed carried pistols—and swords and knives and God knew what else—and had the man not been a Puritan, she was sure one or both of them would have jumped to his defense. But because of men like this one, Jason had been left to raise his orphaned siblings, all of them forced to spend the Commonwealth years in poverty and exile.

She turned to watch the amber man remount and make his way down the road and up the hill toward his cohorts. He'd been superb. Magnificent.

Romantic, she thought on a sigh.

Amber. His clean-shaven, suntanned complexion. His eyes, a deep gold the color of the finest liquor. The black plume on his cavalier's hat fluttered as he rode, and beneath it he wore a long, crimped brown periwig that rather reminded her of her twin Ford's hair. But she was certain the highwayman's real hair wasn't brown. Though many men had shaven heads under their periwigs, he wouldn't. His own hair would be cut short, but not *off*, certainly—she shuddered at the thought—and it would be golden. Amber.

"Are thee going to let him get away with this?" the Puritan demanded, clambering up and glaring at her brothers with their rapiers at their sides.

One of Jason's black brows rose, and he spoke for them both. "I expect so."

The coach lurched and they continued on, but the atmosphere was decidedly strained, and the Puritan got off at the next stop.

Kendra moved to sit in the now-vacant spot beside Ford. "A highwayman," she breathed as soon as the carriage resumed moving.

"Why didn't he rob us?" Caithren asked. "How is it you know him? He called you a friend."

"He uses the term lightly." Jason's smile was enigmatic. "We've run into him before. But he's never robbed us."

"He didn't look like he needed to rob anybody," Kendra pointed out. "His suit was nicer than yours."

He'd looked nicer than Jason all around, she mused. Not that Jason wasn't handsome, but he had the general look of her family, a look she was inured to, to say the least. This man, on the other hand, had looked...exotic. All golden and dressed in black—black suit, black shirt, black boots, black mask—not the look of your typical scruffy felon, that was for sure.

Jason shrugged, absently running a hand through his wife's straight, dark-blond hair. "Almost anyone can afford one nice suit of clothes, if he makes it his priority. You cannot judge a man by his looks, Kendra."

But of course she had. Judged him, and liked what she saw.

Jason raised Cait's hand and brushed his lips over her knuckles, earning a soft smile in return. "Perhaps we should turn him in," he suggested playfully. "This is getting to be somewhat of a nuisance."

"You wouldn't dare!" Kendra burst out. "He's... well...he'd fit in at court. And he robbed only the Puritan. I'd wager he's a Royalist."

"There could be a reward for him. And Lakefield House is in sad shape," Viscount Lakefield, otherwise known as Ford, lamented half-seriously. "I cannot live with Jason forever."

"Oh, yes, you can," Kendra said heatedly.

Jason turned to her. "Is it that important to you, then? I didn't realize your Royalist loyalty ran so deep."

"Well...it does," she declared, thinking about the highwayman's broad shoulders.

"Well, then." Ford's deep-blue eyes gleamed with mischief. "I suppose we'll have to leave him be. At least it provides him with a stake for the card games."

Jason glared at their brother.

"What?" Kendra asked. "What card games?"

"All highwaymen play cards," Jason said firmly. He picked up their own deck and shuffled it expertly, then dealt out new hands.

Kendra arranged her cards slowly, her mind not on the game.

She remembered the highwayman's voice. He'd spoken cautiously, as though he were considering each word. Not like her family. The Chases, as a rule, blurted everything that came into their heads, generally at the tops of their lungs.

"What was his accent?" she asked. "Did you hear it?"

"Scots, aye?" Cait said, exaggerating the burr she was born to. "Though I'd guess he hasn't been home for many a year. I'm surprised you even noticed."

When Jason looked up sharply, Kendra pretended to study her fan of cards. He frowned back down at his own hand. "Why do you want to know?"

Why? She could scarcely comprehend such a stupid question. She wanted to know everything about the mysterious highwayman.

"Just curious," she said lightly, leading with a knave of hearts. "Your turn."

KENDRA AWOKE the next morning with a massive headache. Jason couldn't be serious. After her disastrous interview with the Duke of Lechmere, he'd laid down the law: she would be wed by summer's end.

He and Ford and Colin were off to a monthly house party they attended—no females allowed—and when they returned, they'd be expecting to hear whom she'd decided to marry.

She stared up at the underside of the mint-green canopy she'd begged for in her youth. Although their parents had depleted the family fortune financing the king in the Civil War, Jason had always seen to it that she'd never wanted for anything. To the best of his abilities, he'd indulged her every whim. He wouldn't force her to marry now.

Would he?

With a huff, she rose and pulled on her new hunter-green riding habit. She ran a comb through her hair, not bothering to call her maid in to curl and pin it. In no time at all, she was mounted on Pandora, her mare, galloping across the Sussex Downs.

Her brothers would be mightily vexed if they knew she was riding unescorted, but the three of them could go hang for all she cared right now.

Besides, they were away all weekend and would never know.

The fresh country air eased her aching head, but just

thinking about that weasel Lechmere made her shiver. And the rest of her prospects weren't much better.

The Earl of Shrewsbury came complete with a meddling mother—the "shrew" in her title was all too fitting. The Marquess of Rochford was a widower and kind enough, but his hair was completely gray—doubtless from dealing with his seven unruly children. Viscount Davenport didn't talk, he whined. The Duke of Lancashire lived in, well, Lancashire—which was entirely too far from her family. The Earl of Morely was wealthy and wise, but nearing fifty. Lord Rosslyn was young, handsome, and fun loving, but lacking somewhat in brains. She wondered if he could read.

Jason couldn't be serious.

Coming out of her thoughts, she slowed to a stop. She hadn't realized how far she'd ridden. In fact, she noticed with a start, she was at the same spot where they'd seen the highwayman yesterday.

His friends had been atop that hill, lying on their stomachs, their hats pulled down to conceal their faces, training an impressive assortment of pistols on the hapless Puritan.

This morning, the hill was deserted and the highwayman nowhere in sight. In an attempt to judge the time, Kendra glanced at the sky, but it was all clouded over. The day was turning beastly. Not cold, but muggy, with a definite threat of rain. With no sun to confirm it, she guessed the time to be about ten o'clock. Perhaps highwaymen slept in.

Plainly, highway robbery wasn't a full-time occupation. Not that she had any idea of what she'd have done if the highwayman *had* been here. Run for her life, in all probability. But she drifted into a vague fantasy of herself riding down the road at breakneck speed, her long, dark red hair floating on the breeze, impressing the hell out of him with her horsemanship and her grace. In her fantasy he stared after her, openmouthed with surprise and appreciation, struck temporarily dumb by a bolt of…love at first sight.

Well, second sight, actually—but he hadn't paid any attention to her the first time, so surely that didn't count.

Then she would turn around, ride back, stop in the middle of the road, right in front of him, and slide off Pandora slowly…so slowly. Still gazing at her, he'd come forward, reaching her in two or three of his long strides, his large, strong hands spanning her waist as he eased her to the ground. And then…

She had no idea. Inexperience didn't make for detailed fantasies. And she certainly wouldn't have anything to do with a highwayman, anyway. Her fantasy wasn't only boring, it was absurd.

But instead of turning back, she rode along the crest of the hill a spell, then turned away from the lane. And there, perhaps a hundred feet distant, was a very mysterious mound.

It wasn't sculpted by nature, Kendra realized immediately. Its shape was angular, its surface dirt, not grass.

A grave. A fresh grave.

Her hands tightened on the reins as she approached the tomb. Who could be buried there? The highwayman? A victim of his? Either one was unthinkable. She bit the inside of her cheek, worrying the soft flesh with her teeth.

A single raindrop fell on one of her clenched fists, and a gust of wind whooshed as she reached the mound. From her perch atop Pandora, she saw the loose dirt blow across it, revealing a sheet of canvas underneath. Her heart hammered at the sight. Was the man not buried properly, then—just covered with a spot of fabric?

She slid off Pandora and led her forward to investigate. Leaning down, she took a corner of the canvas, just a corner, in two shaking fingers and lifted it…

If her brothers had been here, they'd have told her, as usual, not to jump to conclusions. And this time, they'd have been right. Her shout of laughter rang across the Downs as she threw back the canvas.

Twelve blocks of wood. Twelve narrow pipes of various gauges. Twelve hats with different colored plumes and a variety of hatbands.

She tethered Pandora to a tree. Atop a nearby hill, she set a hat on a block of wood with a pipe sticking out from under it. When she ran back down and glanced up, it looked for all the world like a man lying on his stomach, pointing a gun at her.

He was clever, this man. Very clever.

"What do you think you're doing?"

She froze. She hadn't heard anyone approach, and for the barest second she thought the voice was in her head. But he was standing behind her. She could feel his presence, maybe three feet away.

"I'm…" Words failed her. "I'm…"

"You're letting my hat get wet."

"Oh." Kendra put a hand to her head, feeling the mass of her hair curling with dampness. She hadn't noticed the increasing drizzle. "It's raining."

"Very observant of you."

She turned then and gazed up at him, and he looked exactly the way she'd known he would. His hair *was* golden—thick, silky, and straight. It was cut short, not chin-length like a Puritan's, nor cropped like a wig-wearing Royalist's, but somewhere in between, and the front was hanging in his eyes. She wanted to reach out and sweep it off his forehead, but she seemed rooted in place, and she wouldn't have dared to touch him anyway.

His snug black breeches were wool, not velvet, and his shirt was white, not black. He wasn't here for business, then.

"I've come to save my props from the rain. Will you help me, seeing as you're here?"

Help him? She ought to be bolting for Pandora at this very moment. "Of course."

Had she said that? She knew she shouldn't have. He ran up the hill and snatched up the three props, then turned and strode back to the rest of them. Windblown, his golden hair bounced in time with his steps as she followed.

She concentrated on his broad back, watching the play of muscles beneath his thin shirt as he flipped over the canvas and piled the hats on top, bundling them up and tying the four corners in a neat knot to make a parcel. He hefted it, testing its weight, then turned to her. "You can carry this, aye? Before you, on your horse?"

He didn't sound cross with her, more like he was simply resolved to complete his task in the most efficient manner possible. Kendra was somewhat relieved, but she moved in a haze of unreality.

She managed to find her voice, however. "If you'll hand it up to me, yes, I'm sure I can carry it. Where are we taking it?"

"A cottage over the next hill, not too far." He gathered the pipes under one arm and lifted the bundle by its knot. "Let's be off, before it starts raining in earnest."

His horse was tied by hers—amber, of course, his glossy coat a tawny tan color. Pandora's hide was a deep brown, and Kendra thought they made a handsome pair.

It was difficult to see over the bundle in front of her, but it was a short ride.

The cottage was unlocked, and the highwayman made short work of tethering their horses before depositing the pipes inside and returning for the bundle. After handing it to him, Kendra slid off Pandora slowly…so slowly…and a second later he was back, and his large, strong hands were spanning her waist as he eased her to the ground.

His fingers rested on her waist a little longer than necessary, and she felt their warmth through her habit. She looked up at him. He had a wide mouth, the full lower lip perfectly straight across the center bottom edge. She wanted to touch him, just there.

Her eyes locked on his, and her breath caught in her throat.

A crash of thunder rent the air, and big raindrops began pelting to the earth. He jumped back, motioning her to follow him inside.

She should leave. Now. But it was pouring…

The cottage looked more like a well-appointed hunting lodge, warm and cozy and very masculine. He shut the door behind them and wandered to a leather-upholstered couch, throwing his long form onto it with a surprising grace. "Close, aye? Five more minutes, and my hats would have been ruined. I thank you for your help."

"You're welcome," Kendra said from just inside the

door where she still stood in a daze. She couldn't believe she was in a hunting lodge with this dangerous man. It was incredible—and, all of a sudden, incredibly scary. She couldn't remember ever having been alone with a man, save her brothers. And she didn't know the first thing about this one—except that he was an outlaw.

The fear must have shown on her face, because he sat straight and patted the cushion beside him. "Come here—I don't bite. You'll stay till it stops raining, aye?"

"Aye—I mean, yes." Outlaw or not, she loved the way he talked, the words slow and melodic. Though her heart was pounding, she screwed up her courage and moved to sit gingerly beside him. "I'm Kendra. Kendra Chase."

"Trick Caldwell."

"Trick?" she echoed, startled. She turned to him, forgetting for a moment that he was supposed to be frightening. "What kind of a name is Trick?"

"Ah, and that's a story." He smiled at her, a wide white smile that lit up the cottage and belied the dreary day. Leaning forward, he reached out a hand and placed it on her wrist, just lightly, but a tingle raced up her arm and throughout her body, warming her in the strangest way. Something snapped inside her, and the sense of unreality was gone.

She was here, really here, with the amber highwayman—no, Trick, she corrected herself—alone, and he wasn't scary at all.

Well, not very.

AVAILABLE NOW!

Learn more about *A Duke's Guide to Seducing His Bride* **at**

www.LaurenRoyal.com

ENTER FOR A CHANCE TO WIN
the pearl necklace that
Cameron gives Clarice in this book!*

Visit the Contest page on Lauren's website
at www.LaurenRoyal.com
and answer a question to be
entered in the monthly drawing.

No purchase necessary. See complete rules on the site.

*Please note: Depending on when you enter, the prize may be another piece of
jewelry associated with one of Lauren's books. The author reserves the right to
discontinue this promotion at any time.

ABOUT LAUREN ROYAL

~

LAUREN ROYAL is a *New York Times* and *USA Today* bestselling author of humorous historical romance. Her "truly enchanting" novels have won many awards including *Booklist*'s "Top 10 Romance of the Year" and earned raves from reviewers including *Publishers Weekly*, who calls her "an impressive talent."

All of Lauren's books are complete, stand-alone stories, and yet they are also all connected—because they all feature her beloved "outrageously funny, loyal, compassionate, and unconventional" Chase family.

Lauren writes steamy historical romance on her own and sweet/clean historical romance with her daughter, Devon Royal. She lives in Southern California with her family, their constantly shedding cat, and a stupendous collection of fuzzy socks. When she's not busy writing, she enjoys singing along (off-key) to Hamilton, dancing (badly), and (wasting time) watching HGTV.

·

CONTACT INFORMATION

Lauren's Newsletter

littl.ink / LaurensNews

Facebook Readers Group

facebook.com / groups / ChaseFamilyReaders

Facebook Page

facebook.com / LaurenRoyal

Website

www.LaurenRoyal.com